RETURN OF THE TEXAN

Johnny Canavan was quick on the trigger when injustice was being done. When he rode into the cow-town of Cuero, Texas, he landed smack in the middle of a bloody battle between cattlemen and homesteaders. He fearlessly put his life on the line to protect the helpless homesteaders from the vicious cattlemen who were killing women and children to get what they wanted. In the midst of this feud, he fell in love with a woman—the wife of another man . . .

BURT ARTHUR

RETURN OF THE TEXAN

Complete and Unabridged

LINFORD
Leicester

First published in the U.S.A. in 1956 by
Nordon Publications Inc.

First Large Print Edition
published November 1985

British Library CIP Data

Arthur, Burt
    Return of the Texan.—Large print ed.—
Linford western library
    Rn: Herbert Arthur Shappiro   I. Title
    813′.54[F]   PS3569.H342/

    ISBN 0-7089-6185-1

Published by
F. A. Thorpe (Publishing) Ltd.
Anstey, Leicestershire
Set by Rowland Phototypesetting Ltd.
Bury St. Edmunds, Suffolk
Printed and bound in Great Britain by
T. J. Press (Padstow) Ltd., Padstow, Cornwall

1

THE pin-scratched initials in the heel plate of his low-slung, tied-down gun were "JC." They stood for Johnny Canavan. There were six feet, four inches and two hundred pounds of him, and his weight was perfectly distributed over his broad-shouldered narrow-hipped frame. When he thumbed his dust-streaked hat up from his forehead and let it ride on the back of his head, red hair was revealed crowning his sun-bronzed, bitter-eyed face. Tuck Wells, the balding, celluloid-collared, string-tied and sleeve-gartered bartender, glanced at him again and finally asked the question that he had wanted to ask the very first moment Canavan entered the place.

"Mister, haven't I seen you before?"

Hunched over the curved lip of the glistening bar with his shoulders rounded and his right boot heel hooked over the scuffed footrail, and his big hands wrapped around a half-drained, foam-ringed beer glass, Canavan lifted his eyes to him.

"I mean, you've been in here before, haven't you?"

Canavan nodded and answered:

"Yeah. Long time ago, though."

Wells smiled and said:

"Thought so. That's the way it is with me. Once I see a face, I never forget it. Wish I was that good remembering the names that go with those faces."

Canavan made no response. Wells squeezed out his bar-rag and swished it over the bar.

"Cuero look any different to you since the last time?"

"Haven't had a chance to look around, so I can't tell yet."

"Then I can tell you. Nothing's changed around here. Leastways, not in the ten years that I've been here. 'Course like every place in Texas, a handful o' homesteaders have moved in on us. But so far nothing's come of it, and there hasn't been any trouble."

2

There were voices outside and heavy bootsteps on the veranda, and presently two men appeared and came trooping into the saloon. Wells looked up and greeted them with a half-salute. They glanced in Canavan's direction as they halted at the bar and leaned over it; he didn't look familiar to them, so they looked away.

"Beer, Tuck," one of them called.

"Comin' up," Wells answered and moved away to serve them.

Cuero, Canavan repeated to himself. So that was where he was. Riding into town, he remembered thinking to himself that there was something vaguely familiar about the place, and he took it for granted that he had been there before. But he couldn't recall the town's name, and there were no signposts as there were in most towns to tell him. It was only when the bartender mentioned it that old memories associated with Cuero began to return to him. A band of wanted men, killers all of them, who had outdistanced pursuing lawmen and who had taken refuge in Mexico, and ventured back across the border in a brief show of

3

defiance, and had taken over Cuero. The sheriff had appealed to the Rangers for help, and Cap McDermott had sent Canavan to drive out the intruders. The name of the Cuero sheriff came surging back to him. It was Embree. He wondered if Embree was still around. He probably was, Canavan told himself, remembering that the bartender had said that nothing had changed there, and Canavan assumed that that included the sheriff.

A forced, all-night ride had brought Canavan to Cuero at dawn. Informed of his coming, Embree and his deputy were waiting for Canavan just outside of town. At his insistence, they carried the fight to the lawless, routed them out of bed in the town's only hotel which they had taken over for themselves, and drove them out to the street. In the gun fight that followed, Canavan grimly recalled, he had disposed of two of the intruders and wounded a third one. The wounded man and the other surviving members of the band managed to get to their horses and make their escape in the same direction from which they had come.

That was Canavan's last assignment. Reporting to McDermott by telegraph that he had completed the Cuero assignment, he had asked for orders. McDermott had answered without delay. Canavan, who hadn't had any time off in about a year, was to go on a three weeks' leave. When the leave was over, he was instructed to report at Ranger headquarters in Austin.

Beth, his pretty bride of some thirteen months, had gone to visit her cousins, Ben and Millie Jessup, who lived in Clovis. Beth's letter telling him of it, written just before she left, was in his pocket. Canavan headed for Clovis. It would be a happy surprise for Beth. First, she wouldn't be expecting to see him so soon, and second, she wouldn't have to make the return trip home by herself. But when Canavan arrived at the Jessup place, a frightening scene confronted him. The house had been burned to the ground. What made it worse was the fact that there was no one around to tell him what had happened, to reassure him more than anything else. He raced back to town and burst in upon Clovis' sheriff. Five minutes later he was back in the saddle and drumming downstreet, and an all-consuming rage was burning inside him.

"Didn't know where to get hold o' you, Canavan," the red-faced sheriff had told him lamely. "Or I'da got word to you."

"Why didn't you get in touch with Ranger headquarters?" Canavan had flung back at him. "They'd have known how to reach me."

"'Fraid in all the excitement I didn't think of that."

"What happened?" Canavan had demanded impatiently.

"Well, let's see now. It all started when some nesters moved into the valley. Feller named Millen who bought the Bar-Z spread last winter, he had a run-in with them and he got the other cattlemen down on them, and finally talked them into going after them and chasin' them out. Jessup was the only one who wouldn't take a hand in it. Millen went out to see him and they had some words, then they started throwin' punches at each other. Jessup gave Millen a

6

good walloping, and Millen picked himself up off the ground, told Jessup he'd fix him good for what he'd done and went off. Late that same night . . ."

"Hold it a minute," Canavan commanded. "How d'you know all this?"

"Got it from somebody who was there," the sheriff answered. "That Briggs feller that Jessup had working for him."

"Go on."

"Now where was I?"

"You started to say something about late that same night."

"Oh, yeah! Jessup didn't have any bunkhouse, so Briggs bedded down in the barn, in the hayloft. He woke up when he thought he smelled something burning. He poked his head outta the loft window and saw the house burning. There was a man standing in front of it. When your wife and the Jessups came strumbling out, he plugged them, shot them down."

"Briggs recognized the man?"

"He says it was Millen. There's only one thing wrong with that."

"Yeah? What."

"The barn's some forty, maybe fifty feet from the house. Leastways from where the house was. From that far away and in the dark. . . ."

"The house was burning, so it couldn't have been too dark to recognize and identify somebody standing in front of it."

"Yeah, guess that's right. Now if we could only find Briggs . . ."

"Y'mean he's gone?"

"Yeah. Got some wild idea in his head that Millen and the others might try to kill him so's to close his mouth. So he lit outta here before I could stop him and nobody's seen him since."

"You get a statement or something from him before he hightailed it?"

"Didn't get around to that."

"Swell," Canavan commented bitterly. "What about Millen? You took him in, didn't you?"

"I was gonna, Canavan. Fact is, I even started out for his place. But then I got to thinking, and I turned around and came on back. Y'see if I'da taken him in and brought him into court, with no witness to back up the charge against him . . ."

"I see. Millen still around?"

"Yeah, sure. So are the others who were mixed up with him in this nester business. For my dough, they've all got blood on their hands, every last one of them. But how am I gonna go about getting them convicted?"

"Who are they? The others, I mean."

"There are five o' them. Trauble, Skowron, Quinn, Lang . . . and lemme see now. Oh, yeah, Jake Horton. That make five?"

"Yeah," Canavan replied as he hitched up his pants and headed for the door.

"Wait a minute, Canavan," the sheriff called, pushing back from his desk and getting up on his feet. "Where are you going, and what d'you aim to do?"

Canavan didn't answer. He didn't take the time. He bolted out, dashed across the planked walk to his horse, vaulted up into the saddle and flashed away.

Horton, Lang and Skowron died in the doorways of their homes, shot to death when they came in answer to Canavan's repeated bangings on their doors. Trauble delayed in responding to Canavan's gun-butt door thumping, and the latter, suspecting something, crept around the Trauble house to the front door just as it opened and the cattleman came tiptoeing out. When he spied Canavan, he tried to back inside again. It was too late. Canavan's gun was much too quick for him. A bullet that slammed into his body drove the breath out of him and his thick legs buckled and he fell clumsily on his hands and knees. He forced himself up again, and swaying on rubbery, wobbly legs, struggled to get his own gun out of his hip holster. A second shot struck him and he tottered brokenly and fell and sprawled out and died in a widening pool of his own blood. Quinn, the fifth and last Millen follower, wasn't at home when Canavan pulled up in front of the man's house. So Canavan waited for him to return, hiding in the shadows behind Quinn's house. It was almost midnight when the rancher appeared. Apparently he had learned of the fate that had befallen the others for he sidled up to the house, and staying well within the deep, blanketing shadows he hugged the wall and followed it to the rear. He peered around the house cautiously and, seemingly satisfied that he was safe, stepped up to the door. Canavan watching him, permitted him to unlock and open it before he confronted him.

"All right, Quinn," he said curtly. "Hold it."

Quinn stiffened.

"Turn around," Canavan commanded.

Slowly the cattleman obeyed, but when he squared around, his gun was in his hand. His bullet went wild, ploughing and spewing dirt six feet from where Canavan stood.

Canavan's gun roared an angry reply. Bullet-riddled, Quinn was flung backward into his house. He collided with something that fell with him. The door creaked a little, eased forward on its hinges and, gathering momentum, swung and slammed. Reloading and holstering his gun, Canavan trudged away to his waiting horse. A minute later he was on his way to the Millen place.

Because Millen had done the actual killing, Canavan had left him for the last to be dealt with. Upon Millen's head all the burning rage and the swelling clamor for vengeance would be heaped. Millen's house was shadowy and silent when Canavan rode up to it. The door was unlocked and it yielded to him when he turned the knob. A search of the house, then of the barn, disclosed signs of a hasty, almost frenzied flight. Deciding that his quarry had fled into the nearby hills, Canavan set out after him. It took him two full days before he overtook Millen. Then it became a cat-and-mouse pursuit, with Canavan letting Millen know of his closeness, but never giving the hunted man more than a fleeting glimpse to shoot at. Each time he did, it brought a hastily and wildly fired shot from Millen. Then, on the third day, when there were no more shots from Millen—an indication that his gun was empty—Canavan brought the pursuit to a close.

Millen had holed up in a pile of rocks and boulders. Circling around and coming down upon him from the rear, Canavan swarmed over him, overpowered him, and dragged him out and hauled him to his feet. Gesturing and pushing Millen ahead of him, Canavan herded him up a winding trail that came to an abrupt end at the edge of a rocky ledge. The panting, wheezing Millen stole a quick look behind him; when he saw the valley far below the ledge, he whirled around with a scream and lunged at Canavan wildly, clawing and kicking. Canavan lifted him bodily and with a mighty heave hurled him out over the ledge. Millen's scream trailed after him as he hurtled downward to his death.

Canavan returned to Clovis for a look at the churchyard graves of Millen's three victims. Then he headed for Andersonville, the county seat, where he tried to surrender himself to Arch Trumbull, the County Attorney, who had known him for years. Simply and without embellishments of any kind, he told Trumbull the whole story. Trumbull refused to accept his surrender; he insisted instead that Canavan stay at the Trumbull home while he sought advice from the state capitol on what to do about

Canavan. At the end of the third day, Trumbull brought doughty old Cap McDermott back to the house with him. Canavan was slumped back across the bed in the spare room. He sat up at once, shuttled his questioning gaze between McDermott and Trumbull.

"You're free to go," the latter began, and Canavan's eyes held on him. "The State's Attorney agrees with me that we would never be able to convict you. No jury in the world would ever bring in a verdict against you. So . . ."

He didn't finish. He turned away. McDermott, white-haired and as stiffly erect as a West Pointer, stepped forward then and handed Canavan a folded paper. When he gestured, Canavan unfolded it. He blinked when he read it. It was his discharge from the Rangers.

Canavan's head jerked when a voice said: "How about it, partner?" His eyes lifted. It was the bartender and there was an apologetic smile on his face. "Don't like to bust in on a man when he gets himself lost in his thoughts. But your beer must be flatter'n all get-out by now. How about me puttin' a head on it and kinda freshening it up for you?"

Canavan looked down into his glass.

"No," he said. "This'll do fine the way it is."

Wells' shoulders lifted in a wordless shrug. Canavan drained his glass and put it down again, slapped a silver piece on the bar, hitched up his pants and sauntered out.

It was the evening of the same day. The saloon was crowded, and Tuck Wells was sweating freely as he served his customers, those standing at the bar in some spots two deep, and filled the orders of those occupying the tables in the back room. Tobacco smoke billowed and mushroomed over the bar and settled like a low-hanging cloud. The rich, sweet smell of it clashed with the offensive smell of stale spilt beer. At the far end of the bar, facing the street, Canavan stood alone, hunched over and toying with an empty whiskey glass that he rolled between his hands. He did not look up when a

15

man came striding into the saloon; it was only when a hush fell over the bar that silence, coming on so suddenly, made him raise his eyes. Most of the standees did not move. Only a couple of them did; they stole a quick look over their shoulders at the newcomer, and just as quickly averted their eyes. The man walked to about midway down the length of the bar and tapped another man on the shoulder and stepped back. The second man turned around, backed a little too so that his thrust-back elbows rested on the bar.

"Yeah?" he asked. "Oh, it's you, Fisher!"

"I want to see you a minute, Sturges."

Others turned around then too.

"What's on your mind?" Sturges asked.

The fingers of his right hand flexed and closed, opened again and stayed open and dangled just above the butt of his hipworn gun.

"Yeah?" he asked again, and there was a taunt in his voice.

"I'm giving you fair warning, Sturges," the man named Fisher said evenly.

Straightening up so that he might get a better look at him, Canavan saw that he was younger than Sturges, about average in height and build. He wore no holster; instead his gun was poked down inside the waistband of his pants. "You drive your cattle over my place again and there'll be trouble."

Sturges, dark-complexioned and rather thin-faced, smiled. He glanced at the men nearest him. A couple of them laughed.

"You heard him, Sturges," Canavan heard one man say. "You behave yourself, or instead of us chasin' the nesters away from here, they'll run us off."

"Yeah," Sturges said. "How d'you like that for gall? A lousy nester with a hole in his britches. . . ."

A burly man with burning black eyes and a week's growth of beard on his full, heavy face, who hadn't turned around, said curtly over his thick shoulders:

"Spit in his eye, Sturges. If you don't, I will."

"I'm coming to it, Coley," Sturges replied. "I don't like it when somebody starts threatening me. You'd better get outta here, Fisher. Get out while the getting's still good."

The homesteader did not move. The burly man whom Sturges had called Coley turned around. When he stood erect, he towered over the others at the bar. A scowl had already begun to spread over his face and was darkening it.

"He told you to get outta here, didn't he?" he demanded in a thickening, phlegmy voice. "You're stinkin' up the place. So get out, y'hear?"

Some of the color began to drain out of Fisher's face. There was a curious whitening around his mouth. Instinctively his right hand came up from his side and stopped again when it reached his waist with his gun butt a hand's span away.

"Get out!" Coley roared and took a threatening step toward Fisher.

There was movement, massed movement, behind Canavan. Chairs scraped on the bare wooden floor, an indication that the men who had been sitting in them had gotten up so that they might have a better view of what was developing in front of the bar. Coley leaped suddenly at Fisher, struck him savagely in the face, and the homesteader rocked under the impact of the stunning blow. His legs appeared to be buckling under him. The big man swarmed over him and slugged him viciously, sinking wrist-deep punches into his body and hammering him with mighty, roundhouse rights to the head. Fisher reeled under the merciless beating. He tottered backward and slumped against the side wall and slid down to the floor on his knees with his back bent and his head bowed and sinking. He sank even lower, hunched over helplessly with his head wavering only inches from the floor. When Coley stood over him and drew back his foot to kick him, a heavy hand caught him by the arm, swung him around and flung him away. Careening wildly and unable to stop himself, Coley collided heavily with the bar.

His right hand dropped and clawed for his gun. He jerked it upward clumsily, out of the holster. As the muzzle cleared the thick lip, there was a roar of gunfire, a deafening, ear-shattering clap of thunder, the echo of which caromed off the ceiling and walls and spent itself in ricochet flight. Coley cried out and dropped his gun, and clutched his shattered right wrist with his left hand. Blood spurted through his fingers and ran over both of his hands and dripped on his pants leg. Canavan, holding his gun on him and half crouching, took his eyes off him for an instant and shot a look at the men flanking Coley. No one moved. Canavan straightened up. Slowly, too, he began to back off, swinging his gun in an arc that took in every man facing him. The fire-blackened muzzle seemed to gape and yawn with a widening mouth at the men whom it cowed and held at bay.

"Well?" Canavan demanded. "Anybody else wanna take a hand in this? How about you, Sturges? Gonna back your side-partner's play, or haven't you got the guts?"

Sturges crimsoned, but he did not answer Canavan's taunt. He took careful pains, while Canavan watched, to bring his right hand upward and away from his gun and hold it against his chest. There were heavy footsteps on the veranda and two men, one a little bulkier than the other and a step behind him, and both wearing silver stars pinned to their vests, rushed into the saloon. Canavan, shooting a quick look at them, recognized the man in the lead. It was Embree, the sheriff. The man behind him, he told himself although he didn't recognize him, was probably Embree's deputy. The sheriff stopped abruptly when he saw Canavan with his levelled gun in his hand. His companion, in full panting stride, didn't stop. He piled into the sheriff, trampling him, and Embree pushed him off angrily.

"Doggone it, Giffy!" he sputtered, half turning to his hapless deputy. "Why in blazes don't you watch where you're going? Once you get moving, you're like a stampedin' steer. Maybe more like a wild runnin' buffalo." His head jerked around. "What . . . what's going on here?"

There was no answer. He looked with frowning eyes at Coley, whose hands were dripping blood, shifted his critical gaze across the saloon to Fisher who was sitting on the floor, head raised now, with his back against the wall. There was a blood smear on the homesteader's mouth and blood bubbled in his nostrils. On his cheekbone was an angry-looking scrape from which blood was oozing and trickling down. Canavan shoved his gun down into his holster, wheeled around to Fisher and helped him to his feet, and held him by the arm, steadying him.

"You all right, partner?" Canavan asked him.

Fisher nodded.

"Then let's go."

The homesteader wiped the blood off his lips with his shirt sleeve. He trudged doorward and Canavan followed him. The two lawmen moved aside to let them pass. Embree and Canavan looked squarely at each other, but no sign of recognition passed between them. Fisher led the way down the veranda steps to the wooden walk.

"Where's your horse?" Canavan asked.

"Up the street."

Together they marched up the darkened

street, their boots thumping rhythmically on the warped planks.

"How long have you been out here?" Canavan asked after a brief silence.

"Oh, about six months now."

"And before that?"

"Illinois," was the reply. "I was born and raised there."

"Farmer?"

"Yes. Taught school in between times too."

"Wanna tell you something, Fisher. The next time you take into your head to go after anybody, even if it's only to warn somebody like you did Sturges tonight, don't do it where he's bound to have some of his friends with him. Best you can get out've anything like that will be the worst. You married?"

"Yes."

"Family?"

"Boy of nine."

"Then you've got a lot to stay healthy and alive for. But now you'll have to keep your eyes open for that Coley as well as for Sturges."

"I'm not afraid of Sturges."

"Good for you. A man who scares easily doesn't belong out here."

"And I'll square accounts with that Coley Nye, too."

Canavan nodded.

"Be sure you're up to it, that you've got what it'll take to do the job, before you try tangling with him. Now Sturges, egged on by Nye, will probably go out've his way to annoy you. And Nye will be after you on his own. He'll be looking to take out of you what I did to him." When they came abreast of a hitch rail in front of a darkened store, with a lone, ground-pawing horse tied up at the rail, Fisher stopped. Canavan halted too. The homesteader stepped down into the dirt gutter and, as Canavan watched, untied his horse. "Little too early for me to be turning in. If you wanna wait a minute, I'll get my horse and ride out to your place with you."

"Fine," Fisher responded.

A cold, chilling wind had begun to blow by the time they reached Fisher's place. The

24

homesteader, apparently finding it difficult to express his thanks to Canavan for having interceded in his behalf, tried to show his appreciation in another way. He prevailed upon Canavan to stay over for the night. But because the house was small and its accommodations limited, Canavan, while accepting Fisher's invitation, insisted upon bedding down in the hayloft in the barn. It wasn't Fisher's idea of hospitality and he argued against it. However, because Canavan insisted that he would have it no other way, the homesteader agreed.

Now it was hours later, nearly midnight, and the house, actually a cabin with a wing added to it, lay steeped in deep darkness. The barn too was shrouded in darkness. Canavan, blanket-wrapped, sat at the open hayloft window, staring out into the night. Twice he had lain down, rolled up in his blanket, but sleep had refused to come to him. He tossed and turned, and he burrowed deeper and deeper in the blanket in his efforts to induce sleep. When it continued to elude him, he finally arose with a heavy sigh, and with the blanket bunched

25

together in his arms, groped his way to the window and forced it open and poked his head out. The wind swirled and droned with an almost human voice. His hand brushed a box that was standing close by and he reached for it and brought it closer, upended it, and flipping open the blanket and draping it around him, perched himself on the box. Resting his folded arms on the window sill, he hunched over it. He raised up a bit and drew the blanket higher and promptly sank down again.

Huddling in the blanket with his mouth and chin buried in a warm, protective fold, he listened to the sounds that arose from the lower floor. Canavan's mare Aggie and Fisher's horse were occupying adjoining stalls. Aggie was the noisier of the two, and was responsible for whatever sounds came from the barn. Canavan knew her whinny, recognized it at once. She stamped on the floor boards each time the wind flung dust against the closed doors. Sometimes her whinny sounded more like a trumpeting, as though she were chiding the wind and the dust for their inability to penetrate the barn. Once or twice Canavan thumped the floor with his boot heel, a warning to Aggie to quiet down, but she disregarded it.

Time passed, the night wind swelled and the darkness seemed to deepen. Canavan's head began to bow and nod. He raised it and sat back, sighed, and wearily started to get up from the box. He stopped abruptly. He thought he saw a man standing in front of the barn. Canavan blinked and peered down again. He hadn't imagined it. It was a man, and he had a half-raised rifle in his hands. A thin finger of night light suddenly glinted on the barrel, ran along it and vanished in almost the same instant. Then Canavan saw two other men appear, and the first man he had spotted ran to meet them. They came together, and after a brief, hushed conference, they separated, each taking a different approach to the silent house with the rifleman heading straight for the front door and the other two slanting away from each other to reach the sides of the building. Canavan whipped off the blanket and slung it aside, pushed the box away too, wheeled and ran to the ladder, skidding on the hay-strewn floor. He made his way down the rungs to the lower floor. Aggie snorted and stamped and began to back out of her stall. Canavan collided with her, cursed and whacked her, and she cried out indignantly but hastily got out of his way. He reached the double doors, unhooked them and flung them back, and bolted out. There was a sudden burst of gunfire, a woman screamed, and a window-pane shattered and fell in with a crash. Jerking out his gun, Canavan ran houseward.

2

THE man who had posted himself at the front door to prevent the Fishers from breaking out, half turned his head for a quick and probably wondering look when he heard Canavan coming toward him. Spotting the approaching figure, he raised his rifle. But before he could fire, Canavan flung a shot at him, and saw him stagger and topple. Glimpsing a second man on the near side of the house, Canavan swerved toward him. The man fired at him. A whining bullet ripped Canavan's hat off his head; he stopped instinctively and made a futile lunge for his hat, missed it and saw it flutter to the ground just out of reach. He fired twice at the man and cursed when he saw that he had missed. The man began to retreat, yelling something, apparently a warning, to the third man whom Canavan couldn't see, and disappeared around the rear of the house. Canavan came skidding up abreast of it. But instead of pursuing the man, Canavan cut sharply past the front of the house, hurdling a huddled-up, hunched-over body that lay in his path. Rounding the house, he ran full tilt into two men who were coming from the rear. Swinging his gun, he clubbed one man with it, the one nearest him, and felled him, and, swarming over the second man, drove him back against the side wall and held him there, with his gun digging into his body. Canavan reached for his captive's gun, wrestled it out of his hand and slung it away. Then quickly stepping back, he held his gun on the man who was struggling to get up. Canavan bent over him, hauled him to his feet. He swayed a little, evidence that he was still shaken and dazed from the clubbing; when he put out his hand and sought to hold onto Canavan, the latter pushed him off, slammed him back against the wall. Stepping on something hard, Canavan bent down and picked it up. It was the fallen man's gun. Canavan tossed it away, heard some twigs snap and break when it fell in a cluster of brush.

"Stay where you are, you two," he commanded, backing off from them. He cupped his free hand around his mouth and hollered: "All right, Fisher. It's over. You can come out now."

There was a moment's silence, then he heard a bolt scrape, heard the front door open, then there were bootsteps. Turning his head, he saw yellowish lantern light shine eerily over the ground. The bootsteps came closer with the light preceding them. A man appeared, holding a lantern in front of him about shoulder high. A woman clutching a half-raised rifle in her hands followed him.

"Come over here, Fisher," Canavan called. "Want you to take a look at these two mavericks."

The homesteader said something over his shoulder, and the woman stopped. He came on, trudging rather heavy-legged and wearily. Canavan took the lantern from him and held it high, so that the two men backed against the house were well within the circle of light that the lantern cast off.

"Know them?" Canavan asked.

Fisher peered hard at them, and shook his head.

"Ever see them before?"

"No, I don't think so."

Canavan grunted, lowered the lantern and handed it back to Fisher.

"All right, you two," he said curtly. "Who put you up to this?"

There was no answer.

"Who d'you work for?"

One of the men cleared his throat, but that was all.

"Get some rope," Canavan said, addressing Fisher, "so we can tie them up."

The homesteader trudged off. When he came to where the woman was standing, he handed her the lantern, and tramped away. He returned shortly with a couple of cut pieces of rope dangling from his hand.

"Turn around," Canavan ordered. "Face the wall."

The two men obeyed. Fisher passed the rope to Canavan, walked to his wife's side and took the rifle from her. Canavan beckoned and he came forward again and held the rifle on the prisoners. As Canavan stepped up to them, Fisher said:

"That man in front of the house. Do we have to leave him there?"

Canavan stopped, looked at him and answered:

"Forgot about him."

He stepped back again, bunched the rope together in the hollow of his left arm and, drawing his gun, said: "Turn around, you men." The captured raiders obeyed. "Let's go."

Canavan herded them ahead of him around the house to where the dead man lay.

"Take him down to the barn," he ordered.

With one man holding him by the feet, they carried him away and put him down again in front of the barn. Aggie, standing in the open doorway, poked her head out at them. Fisher, holding the lantern aloft with one hand and carrying the rifle in the other, came trudging down now, too. Canavan ordered the prisoners to put their hands behind them, and lashed each man's wrists

33

together. When they started into the barn at Canavan's instance, Aggie backed inside to permit them to enter. Each man's ankles were tied together, and each sank down on the floor. Canavan stood for a moment, looking down at them, then he turned on his heel and went out.

"In the morning we'll take them into town," Canavan told Fisher, "and turn them over to the sheriff."

"Right."

"Meanwhile you might as well trot back to the house and go back to sleep."

"What about you?"

"That's what I aim to do, too. I'll leave it to that mare o' mine to see that our friends inside don't get ideas. She'll kick their brains out if they try anything."

Once he was curled up again in his blanket, Canavan had no trouble dozing off and sinking into a sound sleep. He awoke with a start though when he heard Aggie whinnying and pawing the barn floor, and he sat up instantly, reaching for his gun at the same time and half drawing it out of his holster. Mechanically, as he sat there listening, his eyes strayed away to the window. It was dawn. He could see light outside; it was beginning to flood the sky. When he heard nothing more from below, he holstered his gun, and slumped down again and lay flat on his back. But he was wide awake then, and after a few minutes he pushed off the blanket, kicked his feet free of it and sat up again. He smoothed his hair back with his hands and climbed to his feet. There was a stiffness in his body that he attributed to the hard floor and the thin, worn blanket. He rubbed his legs and thighs and when he felt the blood begin to surge through them he lifted and hunched his shoulders and worked his arms about in a punching motion till the stiffness went out of them.

He went down the ladder to the lower floor. The prisoners were where he had left them, sitting on the floor with their backs against the wall. He looked at Aggie. The mare was standing squarely in front of the closed doors, actually against them, blocking them. When Canavan came toward her, she whinnied again, softly though; when he patted her, she nuzzled his arm and shoulder. She backed away from him, a little reluctantly, when he motioned her off. As he opened the doors, he shot a look at the prisoners. Both men hastily averted their eyes. He went outside.

There was a chill in the early morning air. There was an uncomfortable dampishness in it too. When the sun came out, it would burn them away, he told himself. He turned suddenly and started off toward the house, lifting his eyes to it mechanically. The harsh dawn light was anything but flattering to it; it looked uninvitingly drab and makeshift and about as crudely fashioned as anything he had ever seen. But since he had no real interest, his gaze did not hold on it very long. It was his hat that he was looking for. He found it shortly, lying flat and limp and a little dew-damp in the thin crab grass and dirt that fronted the house. He picked it up and turned it around in his hands. He frowned when he saw a black-rimmed bullet hole in the crown. He poked his finger through the hole and muttered something darkly uncomplimentary under his breath about the man who was responsible for the hole. He clapped the hat on his head, and curling the brim, turned and walked back.

He was idling in front of the barn, looking upward and watching the sky brighten, when he heard hoofbeats somewhere off in the distance. They came steadily closer and the drumming beat swelled. He raised his gaze in its direction. Two horsemen came into view. He held his eyes on them, and they, in turn, suddenly spotting him and apparently recognizing him, came on at a quickened pace. One of the men was the sheriff; Canavan recognized him shortly. When they came even closer, Canavan recognized the second man too. It was Embree's trampling deputy. For an instant, Canavan's thought went back to the dawn routing of Cuero's uninvited and unwelcome visitors. Embree and his deputy —whose name still eluded Canavan—were then more of a hindrance than a help. In their excitement they had got in each other's way, and twice, he recalled with a shake of his head, they got in his way too and he had had to hold his fire and give his target a chance to scurry away to cover. It was their failure to cover the backyard and the alleys that flanked the hotel that gave the intruders an avenue of escape. The two lawmen clattered up to the barn, reined in and slacked in their saddles. The deputy was big, hulking and beefy. The look that Canavan had had at the sheriff the night before hadn't told him much about Embree. Now, in the revealing daylight, he could see that Embree had aged considerably since he had seen him last. Embree and Canavan nodded to each other.

"Kinda figured I'd find you out here, Canavan," the sheriff began without any preliminaries. "Looked for you last night after that business with Coley Nye, and when I couldn't find you anywheres around town, I figured you'd come out here with Fisher. Aiming to stay around?"

"Haven't decided yet, Sheriff," Canavan replied. "So I'm afraid I can't tell you."

"Uh-huh," Embree said. "Got a favor to ask of you, Canavan."

"Oh?"

"'Cept for last night, we haven't had any

trouble around here between the cattlemen and the nesters, and we don't want any either. That flare-up between Nye and Fisher, I think I could've smoothed it out between them. Now I don't know. Now I'm not so sure I can do anything. Long as you're around, Nye'll be looking to get square with you for what you did to him, and because of you he's liable to get good and sore at Fisher, and take it out on him. Now if you'd get up on your horse and go on your way so I could see Coley and tell him you've gone . . ."

"Sorry to disappoint you, Sheriff," Canavan said evenly, interrupting him. "But all of a sudden Cuero looks like it might prove interesting to me. So I think I'll stay around for a while. As for your friend Nye, he's way ahead of you. It's too late for you to try to tell him anything. He's showed his hand already. Wanna get down and have a look at what came of it?"

Canavan didn't wait for the sheriff to answer; he trudged around the barn, and Embree, frowning, climbed down from his horse and followed him. But rounding the barn after Canavan he stopped in his tracks and stared hard. In the grass against the side wall lay a canvas-covered body with its booted feet sticking out. Embree gulped and swallowed.

"Who . . . who's that under there?" he asked, gulping again and making a wry face.

"Thought you might be able to tell me," Canavan said. "He and two others tried to raid the place last night. He had the bad luck to get hit. The other two were luckier."

Embree was still staring at the motionless figure. He bent over, lifted a corner of the canvas sheet and peered under it; he lifted it a little higher, bent a little lower and took another and even longer look at the dead man. Suddenly he let the canvas drop, and straightened up.

"Know him, Sheriff?" Canavan asked.

"'Course I know him!" Embree snapped back at him. He began to redden. "God-dammit, Canavan, maybe you don't know what you've done, and maybe you don't care, but you've sure started something.

Something that's liable to turn out to be even bigger than you can handle."

"That so?" Canavan drawled.

"Now there'll be hell to pay, and don't you think there won't! That young feller under that piece o' canvas happens to be a Nye, Lonny Nye, Coley's kid brother, and when Coley hears about this, he'll be fit to be tied. He'll go after you with everything he's got, and take it from me, Canavan, he's got a-plenty, too. Men and guns, and money enough to hire more if he needs them. You take my advice and climb up on your horse and put distance between you and Cuero. If you don't and you find yourself caught in the middle of something, don't look to the law to protect you."

Embree wheeled around and stalked back to his horse.

"Come on, Giffy," he said grumpily. "Let's get away from here."

"Aren't you forgetting something, Sheriff?"

The scowling, fuming sheriff, still a little flushed, looked around at Canavan over his shoulder.

"The dead man," Canavan reminded him.

"You killed him, didn't you? Then you figure out what you oughta do about him."

"All right," Canavan responded. "If that's the way you want it. But if you don't take him with you, you don't get the two who were with him."

Embree thought it over for a moment.

"Where are they?" he asked.

"Got them tied up in the barn."

The sheriff's head turned again. He looked up at his deputy.

"Giffy," he said. "Lonny Nye's layin' around the side of the barn. You oughta be able to handle him by yourself. You make two of him. Boost him up on your horse while I go see about the others."

The deputy didn't look particularly enthused about the job given him. But he climbed down, hitched up his pants and gave Canavan a hard look as he passed him, and trudged away. Canavan followed Embree into the barn. He stood off to a side and watched the sheriff untie the two prisoners and help them to their feet. When

42

Embree led them outside, Canavan turned after them and sauntered out too. The dead man, head, feet and arms dangling, lay slung across the back of Giffy's horse, and the animal kept turning his head and eyeing him with the same doubtful expression that Giffy had worn. The deputy, his chest and shoulders heaving from his exertions, hoisted himself up into the saddle, rested one hand on the dead body in front of him and held the reins in the other hand. Embree mounted his horse.

"You go on ahead, Giffy," he said. "I'll catch up with you."

Giffy grunted; when he nudged his horse into movement, and the animal plodded away, the two Nye hands trudged after him. Embree wheeled around to Canavan.

"Didn't want to say anything about this in front of Giffy," the sheriff began and Canavan looked up at him. "What he doesn't know won't hurt him. But I know about that business up at Clovis, what happened to you and the Rangers, and what you've been doing with yourself since then."

43

Canavan made no response. Embree cleared his throat.

"This drifting around from place to place," he continued, "and never stayin' put anywhere and takin' root isn't good for anybody 'cept maybe an out-and-out saddle tramp. Now why don't you do yourself a favor, Canavan, and go somewhere, some place new, where nobody knows you or anything about you, and make a new start for yourself?"

He rode off suddenly, loped away after Giffy and the two men who were trudging along with him, overtook them and slowed his mount to a walk when he pulled alongside, and went on with them. Canavan, ranging his eyes after them, saw them stop when they came to a clump of the tall brush. Nye's men disappeared behind the brush only to reappear in another minute, mounted and leading a third horse. Embree twisted around and looked back once, squared around again, and the four men rode away.

It was some ten or fifteen minutes later when Canavan heard the front door to the

44

house open, and turning he saw Fisher emerge. The homesteader came striding down to the barn.

"Morning," he said.

"Morning," Canavan responded.

Fisher's face was battered and out of shape. His lips were bruised and puffy, and there was a blue-and-yellowish swelling under his left eye. The scrape on his cheekbone below the eye looked raw and tender.

"The sheriff was here," Canavan told him. "He took the dead man away with him together with the two we caught."

"Was he able to identify the dead man?"

Canavan nodded.

"Yeah. Lonny Nye. Our friend Coley's kid brother."

"Oh," Fisher said, and he looked concerned. "That means trouble, doesn't it? When Nye finds out that his brother was killed here . . ."

"I don't think he'll be after you for that."

"Then he'll be after you."

"That's all right. Let him. I can take care of myself."

"It isn't fair. What you did was in our

behalf, and for you to get into trouble over it . . ."

"Forget it."

The worried look didn't leave Fisher's face, even when he said:

"Breakfast is ready."

"Thanks, but I think I'll wait and have mine when I get to town."

"My wife's expecting you to eat with us. She's set a place for you."

The door opened again and both men looked houseward. A slim, aproned young woman stood in the doorway.

"Breakfast," she called. "Come and get it while it's still hot."

"You see, Canavan?" Fisher asked with a half smile.

"Well, long as she's expecting me . . ."

Together they marched up to the house. Nearing it, Canavan glanced at the shattered window. The frame gaped emptily. Molly Fisher, brown haired and comely, waited in the doorway, holding the door for them. She smiled at Canavan and said:

"We're happy to have you eat with us."

"Thank you," he responded.

She backed inside, holding the door even wider. Canavan took off his hat as he entered the house. Fisher came in behind him, took Canavan's hat from him and hung it next to his own on the back of the door. A table with a bright red checkered cloth that was a little too big for it and that hung rather low over its sides stood in the middle of the room. Three chairs, straight-backed and stiff-looking, were pushed in close to the table. Directly beyond it was the window. Thin rays of sunlight were playing over the narrow sill and sifting inside. Past the window and standing flush with the far wall was a white iron bedstead with a quilt drawn up over it. Canavan's eyes probed the bare wooden floor below the level of the window for signs of broken glass, but there were none. The doorway that separated the room from the wing that had been added was a step or two past the bed and curtain-covered. Since there was no sign of the homesteader's son, Canavan took it for granted that the boy was quartered in the wing and that he was still asleep

47

in there. He glanced at the table again, reminded of it when he recalled what Fisher had told him, and saw that three places had been set.

He moved aside hastily when there was a step behind him. Mrs. Fisher, murmuring "Excuse me, please," brought a fire-blackened coffeepot to the table and a heaped-up platter of biscuits. She followed them with two more platters, one of them holding crisscrossed strips of bacon, the other one piled high with flapjacks from which tiny wisps of steam were still rising and curling. When Fisher placed a pitcher of syrup next to the flapjacks and pulled out a chair and said "Sit down," Canavan nodded and seated himself. Fisher took the chair opposite, and Mrs. Fisher sat down between them. When she said: "All right, Reuben," and bowed her head, Canavan bowed his head too. He caught brief snatches, sometimes only a word or two here and there of Fisher's murmured prayer. When it was finished and he heard the Fishers' chairs creak, he raised his head and sat back. Mrs. Fisher served him some bacon and her husband shifted a stack of flapjacks from the platter to Canavan's plate.

"We're indebted to you, Mr. Canavan," Mrs. Fisher said as he began to eat. He lifted his eyes to her. "I don't know what we'd have done last night if it hadn't been for you. We probably wouldn't be alive now. Then too, Reuben's told me about the fight in the saloon, and what you did for him there. So we're doubly indebted and doubly grateful to you."

"The coffee smells awf'lly good," Canavan answered. "And I'll go outta my way any time for good coffee. If yours tastes as good as it smells, we'll be even."

She smiled and poured the coffee and watched while he sipped his.

"Ah," he said. "Tastes even better than it smells."

There was small talk during the meal and brief periods of silence. Just as they finished, the curtain over the connecting doorway was whisked aside, and a tousled, towheaded little boy appeared and plodded barefooted across the room to his mother's side. She put her arms around him and held him close, smoothed back his rumpled hair, and said to him:

"This is Mr. Canavan, Johnny."

The boy turned in her arms, looked at Canavan and said "H'llo."

"Morning, namesake," Canavan answered.

"Your name is Johnny, too?" Mrs. Fisher asked.

"That's right."

The boy's eyes ranged over Canavan.

"He's awf'lly big, Ma, isn't he?" he asked, half turning to his mother.

"Yes, Mr. Canavan's a big man," she replied. "And you could be just as big as he is if you'd eat everything, as I'm sure Mr. Canavan does."

"I've got a lot of work to do this morning," Fisher announced. He pushed back from the table and got up on his feet. He looked at Canavan. "We'll see you again, won't we?"

"If I'm still around."

Fisher nodded. He drew his gun from inside the waistband of his pants and held it out to his wife. She took it without com-

50

ment and put it in her lap. He crossed the room to the bed, bent down and reached under it and brought out a rifle, and straightened up again. He came back to the table with the rifle slung under his arm. Molly Fisher lifted her eyes to him, and said:

"Be careful, Reuben."

"Oh, I'll be careful, all right," he assured her. "Keep an eye out yourself."

He patted his son on the head and walked to the door, took his hat off the nail on which it had been hanging, opened the door and went out. As it closed behind him, the boy said disappointedly:

"He was gonna take me with him today."

"He'll take you another time, Johnny," Mrs. Fisher told him. She cupped his round little face in her hand and kissed him lightly on the very tip of his nose. When she sought to rub noses with him, he laughed and struggled to break out of her arms, but she held him tight. She finally released him, patted him on the backside and said: "Get dressed, Johnny, and have your breakfast."

He padded away, disappeared behind

the curtain. Canavan's eyes met Mrs. Fisher's.

"I'm so glad he sleeps so soundly," she said with a trace of a smile parting her lips. "He didn't hear anything last night."

Canavan made no response. He had listened without hearing her, listening only to the sound of her voice, not to what she had said. It was a warm, pleasant voice. It made him think of the quiet, rippling water of a woodland brook washing its banks. But there was something strangely familiar about her voice, disturbingly familiar. Suddenly it came to him. He knew what it was. There was so much about her that reminded him of Beth that he stared at her. The resemblance between them was startling, a little frightening also. Their coloring was about the same. Molly was brown haired and brown eyed just as Beth had been. He thought about it for a moment and corrected himself. Beth's hair had had something of a reddish, chestnut tint to it, while Molly's was more decidedly brown. But Beth had worn her hair in just about the same way that Molly was wearing hers.

When she raised her hand to tuck in a straying strand that fluttered before her eyes, he could see Beth doing the same thing and with the same unconscious gracefulness. Like Beth, Molly's skin was smooth and clean and glowed with a healthy pink.

The longer he looked at Fisher's wife, the more it hurt him. He was so starved for Beth, and Molly looked so much like her, it was all he could do to keep himself in check when everything inside of him clamored for her, and the urge to reach out for her began to mount alarmingly. He had to get away from there, he told himself. His hands were clammy. He put them on the edge of the table and pushed back. He stopped abruptly when he heard her say in a tone that was both sad and musing:

"This being a homesteader isn't a way of life that I'd recommend to anyone. It's particularly hard on little Johnny because he's too young to understand. No one to play with, no one to do the things with him that he'd like to do. His father doesn't have the time. A farmer's time is never his own.

A boy as young as Johnny needs companionship, his father's most of all. And when his father can't give it to him, the boy feels neglected, deprived of something that should be rightfully his. His father in turn feels cheated because he doesn't get the opportunity to enjoy his young son. It's different with a little girl. There are dreams and dolls to occupy her time. And when she tires of them, there's always her mother to help her to while away those in-between times. Reuben would have taken Johnny with him today as he promised. But in view of things, he thought it best for me to keep Johnny at home, close by."

Canavan nodded understandingly.

"We didn't have very much in Illinois," she went on. "But we were happy there. And we slept nights. We didn't have to worry for fear that someone might try to steal up on us in the middle of the night and put a torch to our house." Now there was bitterness in her voice, and he could see it in her eyes too. "Here we're outcasts, scorned and unwanted, hated. No one comes near us or wants anything to do with us. And the women. They're just as cruel as their menfolk. The few times I've gone to town, they've cut me, turned their backs on me or walked away when they saw me coming down the street. Even the storekeepers. They don't want our trade. I thought Texas would be wonderful for us. The very place for us. Texas with its vastness and its unlimited opportunities. The promised land. That's why I persuaded Reuben to give up what we had and come out here. This was where we were going to make a new and better life for ourselves. But now that we're here, now that we've seen Texas, now that we've sampled what Texas has to offer, it isn't at all what I had hoped for. It's big, all right. But it's people aren't. They're little people, petty and narrow-minded, and they're mean and cruel, too. I hate Texas. I wish I'd never heard of Texas."

There was a sudden, startling, frightening burst of gunfire, a drumming volley of shots not close by but somewhat distant, and yet not too far off, for the echoes of the shots carried quite clearly in the brisk morning air. Molly stiffened. The blood drained out of her face, leaving it chalky white.

"Reuben," she said, and she stood up.

The gun spilled out of her lap and fell on the floor. She looked down at it, stared at it; she bent suddenly and snatched it up, and with a cry ran to the door. But Canavan was there ahead of her, blocking it.

"Let me out," she sobbed brokenly. "Let me out!"

"No," he said, still barring the way. "That's probably just what they'd like you to do. Run out so they can get you, too. Well, we'll fool them. I'll go. But I won't go till you've gotten hold of yourself. You've still got the boy to think of and take care of. You've got to be strong for his sake. Now how about it?"

She stepped back. He turned and opened the door, stopped astride the threshold and looked back at her searchingly. Her cheeks were tear-streaked, but her sobbing had ceased.

"All right?" he asked.

"Yes," she replied. "I'm all right now."

"Just one thing," he told her. "Want you

to stay put in here. That means you don't even poke your head outside for a quick look. And stay away from the window too. Y'hear?"

She nodded. Her jerked out his gun as he backed out of the doorway. He reached in, curled his hand around the door handle and pulled it to him. Then in full running stride he dashed around the house.

3

CANAVAN stumbled to an awkward, panting stop when he spied a body that he knew at once had to be Reuben Fisher's lying face downward some thirty feet away in a plowed field. He could even see Fisher's rifle. It lay mutely on the ground just beyond the fallen man's reach. But he did not rush on to Fisher's side. Instead, suspecting that the man who had shot him down might still be around, crouching behind cover somewhere close by and waiting in hopes of getting a shot at another member of the homesteader's family. Canavan circled around warily. However, a hasty search of some thin brush that fringed the field, the only cover available to Fisher's attacker, failed to flush out anyone.

Holstering his gun when he was satisfied that the man had fled, Canavan ran back to where Fisher lay motionless. He eased

Fisher over on his back and went over him expertly. Ten minutes later he was trudging back to the house with the unconscious homesteader slung over his shoulder like a bag of meal, and with Fisher's caught-up rifle clutched in his free hand. A couple of times Canavan stopped and looked back, but there was no sign of anyone, and he went on again.

"Molly!" he hollered as he neared the house.

There was instant response. He heard the door fling open, heard quick, running, scurrying footsteps. Molly came dashing around the house, and looking anxiously in his direction, faltered to a breathless, hesitant stop.

"It's all right!" he yelled in an effort to allay her fears. "Open the bed and heat up some water!"

She started toward him mechanically. He waved her off with the rifle, and she halted, suddenly spun around, and darted back to the house. When he rounded it and came up to the door, he found it open. Young Johnny, wide-eyed and a little open-

mouthed and staring up at him, was holding the door for him. Molly came forward at
once. She looked at the limp form of her
husband, and she paled.

"Is he . . . is he . . . dead?"

"Nope," Canavan answered, and he
handed her the rifle. He passed Johnny and
he heard the door close. "Knocked unconscious, but that's all. Lucky for him, he's
got a hard head. Bullet hit him just over the
left ear and glanced off the temple, and
aside from diggin' some flesh and some hair
out've his head, that's all the hurt it did."

He took his eyes from Molly and looked
across the room. She had opened the bed.
The quilt, thrown back, was hanging over
the lower part of the bedstead and trailing
on the floor. Canavan, tramping over to the
bed, reached up and eased his burden off
his shoulder, and half twisting with Fisher
in his arms he gently lowered him and laid
him on the bed.

"Got the water on the fire?" Canavan
asked as he bent over Fisher and began to
take off the man's boots. They were scuffed
and worn and run-down at the heels. He

shook his head when he saw their shabby condition.

Molly came up to the bed.

"The water should be hot in another minute," she said.

She bent over her husband and peered at him anxiously. There was blood on his ear and cheek; peering a little closer she saw that the hair above the ear was blood-matted.

"Didn't take the time out there to clean him up any," Canavan told her. "Wanted to get him back in here soon's I could so we could fix him up. You wanna see about that water now? Oh, I'm gonna need some clean rags, too. Think you can dig up some?"

She turned away without answering. Canavan put Fisher's boots on the floor, pushed them under the bed in order to get them out of the way. He lifted the lamp off the chair that stood next to the bed and put it on the floor, backed against the wall under the paneless window. When Molly returned carrying a pot of steaming hot water, he pointed to the chair and she put the pot on it. She handed him a torn-off piece of a bed-sheet, and he ripped it into small strips. He wound the end of one strip around his finger, dabbed it into the water, and again bent over Fisher. Gently he washed away the blood. There was no sound from the homesteader till Canavan began to clean out the wound, a three-inch furrow in torn, raw, bleeding flesh. Fisher moaned once, and Molly promptly put her hand against her mouth to stifle the cry that came sweeping upward within her. Minutes later, when the wound was thoroughly cleansed and bandaged and Fisher lay still again, Canavan straightened up. Molly drew up the quilt and tucked it in around her husband. Johnny, still wide-eyed, stood near the foot of the bed, looking on.

He tugged at Canavan's sleeve and the latter looked down at him.

"Will he be all right now?" the boy whispered.

Canavan smiled and nodded and patted the boy and walked to the table, pulled out a chair and swung it around and straddled it. When Molly removed the pot of water,

Johnny brought the chair a little closer to the bed and perched himself on it, and sat looking down at his father.

"Is there anything else to do?" Molly asked, stopping at the table.

Canavan shook his head.

"Nope," he replied. "Now all he needs is some rest. He'll wake up with a splitting headache, but it'll pass and he'll be himself again."

Johnny climbed down from the chair and came across the room to his mother's side.

"You gonna stay here now till my father feels better?" he asked.

"Want me to?"

The boy nodded.

"All right," Canavan told him gravely, and Johnny went back to his bedside chair, hoisted himself up and, curling his sturdy little legs under him, sat cross-legged, resuming his vigil over his father. From time to time he hunched forward and peered hard at him; each time, he eased back and sat hands clasped. When he looked up and met his mother's eyes, he exchanged a wan smile with her, and promptly looked away again.

It was the middle of the morning when Canavan loped into Cuero. A halted wagon —whose driver had climbed down to recover a bag of meal that had toppled off—was blocking the way, and Canavan had to wheel wide around it. Passing it, he slowed Aggie to a trot and rode on downstreet. He poked a finger inside his shirt pocket; the list of grocery items that he had come to Cuero to get for the Fishers was still there. Passersby, women as well as men, glanced at him as he came abreast of them, but he ignored them and their questioning stares. Nearing a place with a sign that read EATS swinging out over the walk from above its doorway, Canavan took note of a bulky man who was idling at the curb in front of it. It was Giffy, Embree's deputy, hands jammed deep in the back pockets of his pants, legs slightly spread apart, and rocking a bit on his boot heels. Giffy looked up at him, but Canavan disregarded him and trotted past. He was looking for Shotten's General

Store, and when he spied it farther down the street he headed for it at a somewhat quickened pace, drummed up to it and pulled in at the hitch rail and dismounted. He tied up the mare and stepped up on the walk and tramped across it and went into the store. A stocky, aproned man whom he assumed was Shotten, with a shiny bald head and a fringe of uncombed grey hair ringing his bald pate, was behind the counter, bent over it, adding up a column of figures in a worn and well-thumbed ledger, and posting the total at the foot of the column with a stub of a pencil. He heard Canavan's step and he said without looking up:

"Be right with you."

Canavan grunted, took out Molly's list and laid it on the counter and waited. Shotten put the pencil in his apron pocket, closed the ledger and pushed it aside, and looked up. Canavan pointed mutely to the list, and Shotten said "Oh," and picked it up. He ranged his eyes over it.

"Who's this for, Mister?"

"Make any difference to you who it's for

long as you get paid for it?" Canavan countered.

Shotten flushed a little.

"No," he answered, and hastily added: "'Course not."

Because Shotten had been particularly rude to Molly, refusing to serve her and then ordering her out of his place, Canavan had chosen his store to make the purchases.

"Don't mind telling you though," he added deliberately. "It's for some folks named Fisher."

Shotten lifted his eyes to him.

"Fisher?" he repeated.

"That's right. They're nesters."

"Oh," Shotten said. He held out the slip of paper to Canavan. "You'd better take this somewhere else."

Canavan smiled and shook his head.

"Nope," he said evenly. "You've got what I want, so I'm buying the stuff from you."

"Sorry," the storekeeper said, and he put the slip on the counter and turned away.

Canavan lunged across the counter. He caught Shotten by the arm and flung him

66

around, grabbed him by the shirt front and dragged him back, holding him against the counter, half bent over it.

"I'll give you two minutes to get busy on that order," Canavan told him, his own grim face barely an inch from Shotten's paling face. Beads of sweat broke out over the storekeeper's forehead. "Now if you know when you're well off . . ."

He didn't finish. He released Shotten and the storekeeper snatched up Molly's list and hurried to the rear of the store. He caught up a gunny sack from atop a pile of them and brought it to the counter and hurried off again. He made a dozen trips back and forth, adding packages and bags to the swelling contents of the sack. Then, when he had gotten everything, he produced his pencil stub and listed the prices next to the items, totaled them, and announced:

"Comes to three dollars even."

Canavan slapped three silver dollars on the counter. As he reached for the sack and curled his hand around the open end, he told Shotten:

"Wanna give you a tip, Mister. Next time Mrs. Fisher comes in here, you keep a civil tongue in your head, and you take care of her same's you would anybody else. If you don't, and I have to come back here to show you the error of your ways, it'll be too bad for you. Now that's a promise, and you'd better remember it. Oh, gimme a piece o' rope so I can tie this thing together."

He spied a cut piece of rope lying atop a barrel a step or two away and he reached for it, caught it up, and looped it around the open end of the sack, slip-knotted it, and yanked the rope tight. He hoisted the sack to his shoulder and walked to the door. Halting in the doorway, he looked back at Shotten and said:

"Here's something else for you to think about, Shotten. And if you have any doubts about it, you can ask the sheriff. The law says you have to sell your merchandise, not just you but every storekeeper, to anybody who wants to buy it, providing of course they've got the dough to pay for it. Now you decide for yourself what you want to do,

whether you want to go along with the law
and do what it says, or do what the cattlemen tell you to do and buck the law and
refuse to sell nesters."

He marched out to the curb, slung the
sack over Aggie's back and whipped the
loose end of the rope around the saddlehorn, knotted it, and let the sack hang from
the horn. It thumped gently against the
mare's belly. She turned her head and eyed
it critically, and Canavan said curtly:

"All right now, Aggie. It's just a sack.
You've seen one before, so don't look at it as
though it was something new."

He untied the mare and climbed up
astride her, backed her away from the rail,
wheeled her and rode off. There was no sign
now of Giffy. Canavan's lip curled a little.

"Had to go rushin' back to the office to
report to Embree that I'm in town," he
muttered to himself. "Probably spoiled
Embree's whole day for him."

Nearing the saloon, he saw Tuck Wells
come out to the doorway and flush down the
veranda with a bucket of water. They exchanged half-salutes when Canavan came

abreast of the place. Squaring back again in the saddle as he rode by, Canavan glimpsed a man peering out at him from the entrance to an alleyway some thirty feet away. He wondered about it. When the man withdrew his head, Canavan frowned. But he held his gaze to the spot, watchful for anything more of a suspicious nature. He saw a rifle muzzle poked out at him, and when it levelled he ducked instinctively. The rifle cracked. A bullet whined by overhead, and Aggie stopped dead in her tracks. Canavan's gun was in his hand, half raised for an answering shot. The moment the rifleman stepped out of the alley for a quick look in Canavan's direction, the latter's gun thundered angrily. The man dropped his rifle. It fell at his feet, thumping hollowly on the planked walk. He lurched out to the curb and swayed over it, and when his legs suddenly gave way under him and buckled, his body seemed to arch forward, and he fell limply in the gutter.

There was almost instant reaction to the shooting. Wide-eyed men and women appeared in doorways on both sides of the street. They stared at the hunched-over figure in the gutter, then they lifted their wide eyes to Canavan. He was holstering his gun when he heard a door slam somewhere beyond him; there was a sudden rush of booted feet behind him, and he stole a quick look over his shoulder. Two men, Embree and Giffy, came running up the street. Aggie, not yet over the startling effect of the rifle shot and the uncomfortable nearness of it, backed and pawed the ground and snorted. She subsided, save for an occasional tossing of her head, when Canavan jerked the reins and spoke sharply to her. Embree jumped down into the gutter and cut diagonally toward Canavan, while Giffy ran on to where the fallen rifleman lay. Embree panted to a stop at Canavan's side.

"What . . . what happened?" he wheezed.

"Somebody took a shot at me from an alley," Canavan told him. "That's the one who did it." He pointed to the man. "That feller layin' in the gutter. He missed, but I didn't."

"If you'da done like I asked you, this wouldn't have happened."

"We gonna go into that again? Somebody laid for Fisher this morning and pot-shotted him too."

"They hit him?"

"Creased his skull for him."

"Long as they didn't kill him. But gettin' back to you, Canavan . . ."

"Let's get this settled once and for all, Embree. Nobody's running me out've Cuero. That clear? When I'm ready to go, I'll go, but not before and not because you and your friend Nye want me to. Maybe you'd better tell that to Nye 'less he doesn't care if he runs out've men."

"You're just beggin' for trouble, aren't you?"

"Nope," Canavan answered calmly. "You won't believe this, Sheriff, but I'm downright peaceable. What's more, and I know damned well you won't believe this either, but I shy away from trouble ordinarily."

"H'm," Embree said, plainly not impressed.

"'Course," Canavan went on, "when it comes my way, I don't turn tail and run."

There was no comment this time from the sheriff.

"Here's something else you'd better tell Nye. So far he's been doing all the hitting at me. When I think I've had enough of it, that'll be it. That's when the boot'll be on the other foot. That's when Mister Nye'd better watch out for himself because I'll be after him."

Canavan lifted his eyes, ranged them upstreet. A crowd had formed around the fallen man, shutting him off from view. Two men carrying a sturdy plank came trudging out of an alley, the same one from which Canavan had been fired upon. The crowd opened before them, moved back, and Canavan saw the dead man lifted and laid on the plank and carried away. Then a man with an ankle-length apron flapping around his feet came out of a store with a bucket of water swinging from his hand. Some of the water sloshed over him and he hastily held the bucket higher and a little farther away from him. The onlookers gave

73

way before him, retreated to the opposite side of the street. Standing on the curb from which the rifleman had toppled, the storekeeper flushed the spot on which he had died.

Canavan nudged the mare and she moved off at a trot, leaving Embree standing in the gutter and following Canavan with frowning eyes. Hostile eyes were raised to Canavan as he neared them, came abreast of them and rode past without even a glance in their direction.

It was just after nine o'clock. The night was clear and moonlit, the air brisk. Canavan was idling in front of the Fisher barn, backed against the building a couple of steps past the door. He could hear Aggie moving about inside, stamping and pawing the floor and bumping the stall walls. He shook his head. Something of him had rubbed off on her. He had to exhaust himself before he was able to sleep; apparently it was the same way with Aggie. He turned his gaze on the house. There was no sign of a light there. He had boarded up the shattered window that afternoon, and now he wondered if he hadn't done too good a job of it. Just as he was about to shift his gaze, he heard the front door open and he straightened up. A shadowy figure that he recognized at once as Molly Fisher emerged and stood in front of the house for a minute, then sauntered about, stopping every now and then to look skyward, and once toward the barn. He started for the house, slowing his step when he saw her coming toward him. They came together shortly.

"Thought you folks had turned in," Canavan remarked.

"I've been sewing," Molly told him. "When I finished, I decided to get a breath of air before I went to bed. It's a beautiful night, isn't it?"

"Yes. Reuben all right?"

"He's fast asleep."

"The better he sleeps, the better he'll feel. By morning he oughta feel all caught up with himself."

Together they walked toward the barn.

"Reuben put that up?" Canavan asked.

"What? Oh, the barn? No. It was here

when he got here. It was in pretty bad shape though. Looked as though it was about ready to fall down. Reuben had to do quite a lot of work on it to make it usable. One day he hopes to paint it."

"Uh-huh."

"The house was here, too. But it was hardly more than a shack. We lived in our wagon while Reuben made it habitable. It still needs some work done on it. But I suppose that will be done in time. If we're still alive by then. Canavan, what do you do for a living?"

"I don't do anything," he replied. "Fact is, I haven't done anything these last few years. Just wandered around."

"That isn't much of a life, is it?"

"No."

"Doesn't it get tiresome?"

"Yeah, it does."

"Then why don't you do something about it?"

"Can't. I'm too restless. Can't stay put anywhere for long. Have to be on the move. That's why I can't take a job."

"But a man has to take root somewhere

and grow, doesn't he? That's if he hopes to amount to something."

"Yeah. Guess that's right."

"Well?"

His shoulders lifted in a shrug.

"Don't you want to amount to something?" she pressed him.

He didn't answer.

"Don't you want the things that most other men want?" she continued. "A wife, a place of your own?"

"I've had them."

"Oh," she said, a little taken aback. "What . . . what happened to them?"

"Lost them. That is, I lost my wife and I gave up the place."

"Oh," she said again, inadequately.

"When she died, just about everything inside o' me died too. Since then nothing's mattered. Chances are nothing ever will matter again."

They halted unconsciously when they came to the barn.

"Had you been married very long when it happened?" Molly asked.

"No. Only a little over a year."

"How awful for you! What was she like?"

"She could've passed for your sister."

"Really, Canavan?"

"She looked like you, and sounded like you."

"What was her name?"

"Beth."

"That's a pretty name. It has a nice sound to it."

"Yeah. But there's nothing the matter with Molly that I can see. Look, don't you think you ought to be goin' back inside now? Reuben might wake up sooner than you expect him to, and if he finds you aren't around . . ."

"In a minute. Canavan, I'm sure Beth would be terribly distressed if she knew you'd stopped caring about things, that you'd practically stopped living. Life for the living isn't supposed to end when a loved one dies. The living have to go on living despite their grief. It would be a pretty sorry state of affairs, wouldn't it, if everyone who lost someone simply abandoned all hope and stopped doing whatever it was that he or she had to do? You're still a young man, Canavan. Your life is still ahead of you. It's waiting for you to pick up where you left off and make something of it. And I'm sure you could."

There was no response.

"It would be easier for you than it will be for Reuben."

He looked at her.

"This isn't the kind of life for him. At heart he's a teacher, a man of books, a dreamer. He's a farmer because of necessity, because it's the only way open to him to support his family. His kind wasn't born to fight. It's different with you. You have all the necessary physical attributes for this kind of life. Out here the man who can fight for what he wants, who won't let anyone ride roughshod over him, he's the one who'll make something of himself if he has the will to do it."

He turned his head suddenly and looked in the direction of the house. A man was standing in the open doorway. Turned-down lamplight somewhere behind him silhouetted his figure.

"Reuben," he said quickly.

"Oh," she said and she ranged her eyes after Canavan's. "I hope you aren't angry with me. I know it isn't anyone's business what you do with yourself or with your life. You're the best judge of that. It's just that, well, I don't like to see anyone give up when there's so much to be gotten out of life."

"Molly!" they heard Fisher call. "That you down there in front of the barn?"

"Yes, Reuben!" she answered. "Just getting a breath of air. I'll be along directly!"

She started away toward the house, stopped and half-turning, said:

"Goodnight."

"Goodnight, Molly."

Canavan followed her with his eyes. As she neared the house, Reuben backed a bit, opening the door wider and holding it for her. The lamplight glowed brighter. Presently she was entering the house. The door closed behind her. Canavan backed slowly against the barn.

4

THE next morning when Reuben Fisher summoned Canavan to breakfast, he didn't trudge down to the barn to do it; he stood in the doorway of the house, and when Canavan who was idling in front of the barn and looking skyward happened to turn his gaze on the house, the homesteader beckoned to him. Fisher was still wearing the bandage around his head that Canavan had fashioned for him.

"Morning," Canavan said as he came up to the door. "How's the head?"

"Oh, all right," Fisher answered. "Breakfast is ready. Come in."

Canavan could smell coffee and something baking as he entered. Fisher closed the door after him. This time, though, he didn't take Canavan's hat from him; Canavan hung it on the door nail himself. Molly, bringing the coffeepot to the table, lifted her eyes to Canavan as he turned around, smiled at him and murmured. "Good morning." He smiled back at her. Fisher had already seated himself. "Sit down," he said. Canavan took the same chair that he had occupied before. Molly took her place at the table shortly, too. Canavan was a little surprised when Fisher failed to offer his usual mealtime prayer. The homesteader reached for the bacon, served himself, and pushed the platter back into the middle of the table.

Canavan, glancing at him, wondered to himself, "What's biting him today?" He shook his head when Molly sought to serve him, and she looked at him questioningly.

"Just coffee, thanks," he told her.

"Nonsense," she said. "What kind of a breakfast is that for a man? Give me your plate, please."

"If he isn't hungry, Molly," Fisher said, reaching for a biscuit, "don't force it on him."

There was little conversation after that. There was a noticeable strain, hence the conversation was limited and forced. What little talking there was was done by Molly. Canavan answered when she addressed some of her remarks to him, mostly about the weather, but despite the opportunities she gave him he made no attempt to make any conversation of his own. Fisher finished eating, pushed back from the table and stood up. His wife looked up at him.

"You didn't eat very much, Reuben," she said. "Are you sure you feel all right? Sure you feel up to working today?"

"I feel fine," he replied, rather curtly though, Canavan thought. Fisher walked to the door, lifted his hat off the nail and put it on his head, perching it on top of the bandage and letting it ride there after a futile and apparently painful attempt to pull it down securely. He returned to the table and pushed his chair in close and stood behind it. He looked at Canavan and said: "I suppose you'll be leaving us today."

Canavan met his eyes.

"That's right. I'll be pulling out this morning."

Fisher grunted and strode to the door. His rifle was propped up against the wall just beyond the door. He picked it up and went out. He didn't bother to close the door. He let it swing behind him; it closed and latched by itself. They heard his step outside briefly; as he rounded the house, it faded out.

When Canavan glanced at Molly, there was a faint flush in her cheeks.

"Sure you won't change your mind and eat something?" she asked.

"The coffee was all I wanted this morning," he answered.

"All right," she said with a lift of her shoulders. "Going to town when you leave here?"

"Yes."

"And then?"

"Then I think I'll head out."

"Will we see you again?"

He shook his head.

"But you'll be coming back to Cuero again one day, won't you?"

"No. I think I've had enough of Cuero, and Cuero's probably had enough of me."

She was silent for a long moment, avoiding his eyes. Then she said:

"I want to apologize for Reuben."

"Don't. Every man's allowed to wake up feeling outta sorts every now and then."

"He wasn't even civil to you this morning. It was as though he'd already forgotten how much he owes you."

"Maybe that's what's bothering him."

She raised her eyes; her expression showed that she didn't understand.

"Too much indebtedness can make a man—that is, the one who's indebted—kinda resentful. He can even get to hate the guts of the man he's indebted to. It's happened any number of times. So don't get down on Reuben. He'll come around all right once I'm gone." Canavan got up on his feet. Molly arose too.

"Thanks for everything," he told her with a grave smile. "And say goodbye to the boy for me."

She followed him to the door. He retrieved his hat and put it on and rolled the brim as she watched quietly.

"What are you going to do with yourself, Canavan? What's going to become of you?"

"'Fraid I can't tell you that because I

don't know yet. But don't you go worrying about me. I'll be all right." When he stepped up to the door to open it, she backed off from it. "Bye," he said to her over his shoulder.

She didn't answer. But when he was striding down to the barn, he turned his head and looked back. She was standing motionlessly in the doorway. And minutes later, when he led Aggie out of the barn, she was still standing there, only this time young Johnny was with her. Canavan, bending to tighten Aggie's belly cinch, heard running steps and he eased around on his haunches. Johnny Fisher, running down from the house, skidded to a stop in front of him.

"Hello, son," Canavan said.

"H'llo," the boy responded. "You going away?"

"That's right."

"Do you have to go?"

"'Fraid so, Johnny."

"What's his name?" the boy asked, pointing to the mare.

"It isn't a him. It's a her."

"Oh! Well, what's her name?"

"Aggie," Canavan answered gravely.

"Aggie?" Johnny repeated. "That's a funny name for a horse."

Canavan shrugged.

"That was her mother's name before her."

The boy came up a little closer. Aggie turned her head and looked at him, blinked, and stretching her neck she nuzzled his shoulder.

"Can I ride her?" he asked eagerly.

"Sure."

Canavan reached for him and, straightening up, lifted him off the ground and set him down in the saddle. The mare's head turned again. She eyed the boy perched on her back. Canavan handed him the reins and stepped back.

"All set?" he asked. When the boy nodded, Canavan said, "Go ahead," and added, "Easy, Aggie."

The mare plodded away. Johnny rode in a circle; completing it, he returned to Canavan's side. When the latter nodded, the boy wheeled away, repeated the circle and halted again in front of Canavan.

"Just once more, please?" he begged.

"All right."

"Johnny!" a voice called that Canavan recognized at once, without having to look in its direction to know it was Reuben Fisher's. "Get down, Johnny! Canavan has things to do and you're holding him back!"

"Sorry, partner," Canavan said to the boy.

"Aw, gee," Johnny said grumpily. "Just when I was having such a good time."

Canavan made no comment. He lifted him out of the saddle and put him down on the ground. He curled his left hand around the saddlehorn and pulled himself up on Aggie's back. He wheeled the mare.

"Bye, Johnny," he called over his shoulder as he rode away.

It was still rather early when Canavan loped into Cuero. Drawing rein, he walked Aggie down the street, glanced disinterestedly at a storekeeper who was standing at the curb shaking his broom into the gutter and who looked up when Canavan rode by. The lunchroom farther downstreet was open, and Canavan pulled up in front of it and dismounted, left Aggie idling at the curb, and went inside. There was no one about. But there was movement behind the swinging door that led to the kitchen.

"Be right with you," a man's voice called.

Then the man appeared, pushing through the swinging door. He was a lanky individual with slicked-back hair, blue rosetted garters on the sleeves of his soiled white shirt, a string tie that was frayed and faded, and a stained apron tied around his middle.

He greeted Canavan with a nod and took his place behind the counter. Canavan seated himself on one of the stools, thumbed his hat up from his forehead and hunched over his folded arms.

"Breakfast, Mister?" the lanky man asked, untying his apron, pulling the strings a little tighter around him, and tying them again.

"Yeah."

"Bacon, bacon and eggs, plain eggs, or hot cakes?"

"Which takes the longest to fix?"

"The hot cakes."

"Bacon and eggs."

"Right," the man said, and trudged back into the kitchen. He poked his head out and asked: "Want your coffee now?"

"With the bacon and eggs."

Minutes passed. Still thinking of the Fishers, and disappointed in them because of the way he had had to leave the homestead, Canavan arose and sauntered across the lunchroom floor. The warped boards creaked under him. He stood in the open doorway, with his hands on his hips, staring out moodily. A woman came along, met his eyes, flushed a little and hastily looked away. A man came striding by. He looked hard at Canavan who stared back at him, and the man averted his eyes and quickened his pace. Canavan heard the swinging door squeak and he looked back over his shoulder; when he spied the proprietor peering out at him, he said:

"It's all right, partner. I'm not going anywhere. Just got tired of sitting."

The door squeaked again when the man withdrew his head.

Hoofs drummed upstreet, and Canavan, straddling the threshold, yielded to his curiosity and poked his head out. A horseman appeared and came on at a canter; about midway down the street, he slowed his mouth to a trot. He came steadily closer. Then nearing the lunchroom, he pulled up suddenly when he spotted Canavan; he was motionless for a moment, then he wheeled his horse, and lashing him, sent him pounding upstreet. Canavan saw him reach the far corner, saw him take the westward road in full stride. Backing inside, Canavan's eyebrows arched.

"Wonder what that was all about?" he asked himself.

After a minute he walked back to his stool and straddled it.

"Just about ready, Mister," the lanky man announced from the kitchen. "Gimme about half a minute more."

"All right," Canavan responded. "You've got it."

It was two minutes later when his breakfast was placed before him. He was hungry, hence he made short work of it. Finishing, and squaring back on his stool, he happened to turn his gaze doorward just as someone backed out of it and strode off. He went swiftly to the doorway and peered out, got a glimpse of the retreating figure. It was Giffy. Canavan looked annoyed as he returned to his stool.

"You'd think I was poison or something the way folks around here take one look at me and turn tail," he muttered to himself. "Dunno about that first feller. But I'm willing to bet I know where Giffy went hustling off to. What's more, I'm willing to bet Embree'll be showing up here before I'm done. If he doesn't, I'll be surprised."

He ordered a second cup of coffee, not because he wanted it but because he wanted to give the sheriff time to get to the lunchroom while he was still there. He toyed with the coffee; finally, when it began to look as though he had overestimated the sheriff's concern about him, he sipped it, began to drink it. It couldn't compare with Molly's. Just as he took his last swallow, there was a heavy step. He didn't look around. When a bulky body hoisted itself onto the stool next to his, he knew he hadn't overestimated at all. It was the sheriff.

"Every time I think I'm liable to have some peace and quiet around here," Embree grumbled, "you have to show up."

"Oh, hello, Sheriff," Canavan said. "When did you come in?"

"What brings you to town today?" Embree asked.

"I was afraid that if I stayed away too long, I might get outta touch with things," Canavan answered lightly.

"H'm."

"What do you know that I don't know?"

"When are you pullin' out?"

"Can't quite make up my mind, Embree. First off I thought I might head out today. Now I don't know. Haven't got anything special to do anywhere else, or any place I have to be, so I might as well hang around a while longer and then go."

"Haven't you got any friends you might go and visit?"

"Made the rounds just a couple o'

months ago, so it's too soon to make the circuit again. Don't wanna wear out my welcome, you know."

"I sure wish you had some place to go."

"Mean you're tired of seein' me around so soon?"

"You know doggoned well what I mean and why I want to see you outta here!"

"Maybe that's why I'm stayin' around. Must be some Missouri mule in me. I'm an obstinate cuss."

Embree hoisted himself to his feet. He hitched up his belt.

"Giving up on me so soon?" Canavan asked.

"If you wanna get yourself killed," Embree said angrily, "go ahead. I'm washin' my hands of you."

He turned on his heel and stalked out to the street. Canavan got up, produced a handful of coins, paid for his breakfast and started for the door. He was about a step from it when a rifle cracked and a bullet shattered the front window, spewing pieces and jagged slivers of glass in every direction. Canavan flung himself back toward the side wall, yanking out his gun at the same time. There was a yell from the kitchen, the swinging door was flung open and the lanky proprietor burst out.

"What in blazes . . . ?"

He gulped and stared hard when he saw the window with quivering pieces of glass jutting out of the framework around it.

"Get back!" Canavan barked at him. "Get back before you get your head shot off!"

The man, open mouthed and still staring, slowly turned his head in Canavan's direction. There was a sudden burst of gunfire. Bullets thudded into the corner, into the wall behind it, tearing bits of plaster from it, and into the stools, and the proprietor beat a hasty retreat. On hands and knees, Canavan crawled along the wall to the front door and stole a quick but cautious look outside. He glimpsed two riflemen peering out from an alley diagonally across the street from the lunchroom, and he raised up the barest bit and flung two shots at them and hurriedly backed off again. There was prompt response. Rifle and Colt fire straddled the doorway, riddled and splintered the framework. Spent bullets plowed into the floor. A bullet struck the lamp that hung from the ceiling and shattered the globe. Tiny pieces of glass fell and tinkled on the floor. The proprietor crawled out from the kitchen, hissed, and Canavan looked around at him.

"They after you, those fellers out there?"

"Me?" the lanky man repeated. "What for? I never did anything to anybody. So why should they be after me?"

"You've got me there, partner," Canavan answered. He grinned and added: "Y'think it could be they want to get square with you on account of what they've been eating here?"

"Aw, now . . ."

A swelling of the attackers' fire interrupted the man's reply and sent him scurrying backward to the kitchen. A moment after he backed in under the swinging door, a bullet struck it and splintered it and he yelled in a protest.

There was little opportunity now for Canavan to get in a shot at his attackers unless he was willing to offer himself as a target, hence he huddled low in a corner, fretting and debating with himself as to what he should do. The suspicion that had been growing in his mind with the first shot was now full-grown. Now he knew why the horseman had ridden off so hurriedly after he had spotted him. He was one of Coley Nye's hands. Informed that he, Canavan, was in Cuero, Nye had seized upon the information and the opportunity to square accounts with Canavan. Hastily assembling his outfit, he had despatched it to Cuero. Canavan was sure that Nye's instructions to his men were as final as death itself, a "get him or else" order.

The attackers' fire continued, swelling for a moment and then falling off, and promptly picking up again. The pattern of the fire was simplicity itself. It swept across the lunchroom, from wall to wall, leaving nothing in its wake untouched. The counter and the stools were wrecked; the walls behind and beyond the counter were torn to bits, the plaster shot off and the boards that formed the walls riddled and splintered.

The swinging door was subjected to a withering blast that split it in two. One half broke off of its own weight and fell to the floor, and dust boiled up around it; another burst of gunfire tore the remaining half off its hinges and dropped it on top of the first half.

"Hey, Mac!" Canavan yelled above the din of the shooting.

"Yeah?" the proprietor yelled back. "You want me?"

"I think they're building up to rushing the place," Canavan told him. "Got a back door?"

"Yeah, sure!"

"Then you'd better use it!"

"What about you?"

"I'll be out right after you!"

"Think I oughta go now?"

"Yes! While the going's still good!"

"I'm going! So long, Mister. Hope you make it too!"

"So do I," Canavan muttered half-aloud. He inched over the floor to the doorway, poked his gun out and emptied it in a blind burst of gunfire. Then hastily backing away, he reloaded his gun. He backed into the kitchen on his hands and knees, twisted around when he reached the door and got up on his feet. Shifting his gun to his left hand, he curled his right around the door knob and turned it. The door didn't open.

"What the . . . ?"

He tried it a second time; this time, because he pulled hard on the turning knob, the door opened, but only the barest bit. He peered out through the slot of space. A rope had been twisted around the outer knob to prevent the door from being opened from the inside.

"Why, that lousy son-uva-gun! That miserable . . . !"

He stopped the torrent of angry, bitter words when he realized that he might be blaming the wrong man for shutting off his only avenue of escape. Maybe it wasn't the lanky man's doing. Maybe it was someone else's, a Nye hand who had been posted at the back door to guard against Canavan's breaking out. The man had permitted the lunchroom owner to emerge, then he had sealed off the door with his rope. Canavan was grim-faced when he stepped back from the door. He dropped to the floor instantly when gunfire broke out again and bullets slammed into the walls around him and into the door behind him. He crawled out of the kitchen and crouched behind the end of the shattered counter. After a bit, he sank down on the floor and lay flat on his belly. When he raised his head and peered out, he could see the street.

Suddenly he was concerned about Aggie. There was no sign of her now. He wondered what had become of her. He recalled having left her standing at the curb because there was no hitch rail to tie her to in front of the lunchroom. He decided that she had trotted away of her own accord when the shooting broke out, and he felt relieved.

He saw a man, a bandy-legged, dark-faced man with a half-raised rifle in his hands, come squarely into view directly across the street, step down into the gutter and start to cross. Canavan's gun levelled. It roared suddenly with a deafening clap of thunder, and the man pitched forward and fell on his face with the rifle still clutched in his hands under him. Then two men—a short, stocky man and a tall, gangling mustached and pigeon-toed individual—ran up from the sloping depths of an alley, halted a little breathlessly in the entrance to it, and looked over at the wrecked lunchroom. When one of them, the shorter of the two, said something over his shoulder to the other and started off toward a nearby vacant store, apparently planning to use its doorway for cover, Canavan's Colt voiced a protest. The man stumbled and fell and slumped down on the walk; his companion ran to him and tried to help him up. The fallen man sank lower, and the man with the mustache, sensing that he was beyond help, stepped back from him, jerked out his own gun, and in a show of anger shot twice at the lunchroom. One bullet shattered a glass fragment that was jutting out of the window frame; the second thudded into the counter and spewed tiny bits of splintered wood on the floor. Canavan fired back at him. His bullet caught the man squarely in the chest. He clutched at himself, stared at his hands when he saw them covered with blood; he sagged suddenly and fell head-long over the legs of the first man, and his gun slipped from his numbed hand, slid over the curb and toppled into the gutter.

There was no more shooting after that. The echoes of the gunblasting seemed to hang in the morning air. Gradually, though, they began to lift and fade out. Canavan crawled toward the side wall, reached it and got up on his feet. Half bent over, he inched his way along the wall to the door, sidled up to it and stole a quick look outside. The bandy-legged rifleman who had fallen in the middle of the gutter lay in a widening pool of his own blood. Some of it had already begun to run off and blend with the churned-up dirt. Canavan's eyes searched the alleys and the doorways opposite him for further signs of his attackers, but there were none and he wondered about it, wondered if it meant that they had abandoned the attack without making a converging rush upon the place as he had expected them to do. If they had given up the attack as it appeared, then he didn't think much of Nye's crew. However, he decided to withhold judgment till he knew for certain that they had gone. It might well be, he told himself, that they had withdrawn to discuss some new strategy and that the respite was only temporary.

In the midst of his conjecturing, a woman appeared, seemingly out of nowhere, a woman with a black skirt that looked shiny and worn and a black knitted shawl around her shoulders. Her plain, parted-down-the-middle hair was black but tinged with grey. His gaze held on her. She stopped within a couple of feet of the two men who lay on the walk. She bent a little so that she could see their faces. Slowly she straightened up and looked across the street. She stepped down into the gutter, lifting her skirt to avoid the running-off blood, and halted again when she came to where the rifleman lay. She peered hard at him. Canavan marvelled at her. The sight of blood and of death itself did not appear to affect her.

She crossed the street and came up on the walk in front of the lunchroom and lifted her eyes to it. Canavan couldn't recall when he had seen a plainer face, or one that was so lacking in expression and emotion. Lowered gun in hand, he moved into the doorway. When she suddenly became aware of him standing there, she was neither startled nor surprised.

"You the man they were after?" she asked.

"'Fraid so."

"They've gone," she told him. "All except *them*," and she half turned and indicated the dead men with a wave of a toilworn hand. "What did you do?"

"Well, now, that's a good question, Ma'am," he replied gravely. "I've been asking myself that, but so far I haven't been able to come up with the answer. Leastways, the right one."

"H'm," she said. "You must have done something." She came closer and peered into the lunchroom. "It looks like a tornado hit it. Mr. Squires will be fit to be tied when he sees it."

"Who's Mr. Squires?"

"He owns the bank, and the bank owns this place."

"I see."

"Where . . . where's Mr. Jenks?"

"Don't think I know him, either."

"He runs this place. He owned it once himself. When he couldn't meet the notes, the bank took it over but hired him to run it for them."

"This Jenks a tall, lanky feller?"

"Thought you said you didn't know him?"

"I meant I didn't know him by name."

"Oh," she said.

"He cleared out some time ago."

"What an awful mess," she said with a shake of her head, and walked away.

Now, he noticed, there were other people in the street. The women did not show any desire to view the dead men any too closely, and stood back from them; the men gathered around the three bodies, talked among themselves almost guardedly, Canavan thought, and glanced across the street at him every now and then. Just as he was holstering his gun, he saw Embree and Giffy coming up the street. Canavan eyed them a little scornfully. The two lawmen parted as they neared the lunchroom. Canavan stepped out on the walk. Giffy slanted across the street to where the rifleman lay, while the sheriff, a bit flushed, came striding up to Canavan and said:

"Had yourself a time of it, didn't you?"

"I didn't start it, so don't go blaming it on me. Besides, you're the law around here, or supposed to be. How come you didn't step in and stop it? Or couldn't you and your side-partner get out from under your beds?"

Embree's flush became a deep scarlet.

"Now, just a minute, Canavan," he began sputteringly.

"No," Canavan said curtly. "You wait. One o' those two layin' across the street was one that I handed over to you at Fisher's place. I've been meaning all along to ask you what you'd done about them. Now I know, so I don't have to ask. You turned them loose the minute you got outta my sight that morning, didn't you?"

"I didn't do anything of the kind!" the sheriff retorted heatedly.

"Then how come that feller over there . . ."

"Soon as Nye heard I had two of his hands, he came after them."

"And you handed them over just like that."

"You're wrong about that too."

"Yeah?" Canavan taunted him. "Then why don't you tell me what happened and set me straight?"

"When eight men with guns in their hands come bustin' in on you, you don't argue with them. Not if you've got any sense. You do like they say and you give them what they want."

"But at the same time you told Nye that that wasn't the end of it, didn't you? That the law . . ."

"I didn't tell him anything. I told you I was washin' my hands clean of you and of this mess. If you want to tell him anything, go ahead. Go get yourself shot full o' holes. Maybe then things will quiet down around here and we can go back to living the way we were doing till you showed up and butted into things that weren't any of your business."

"You're quite a lawman, Embree.

You've got no more right wearing that star than . . ."

"Than *you*, maybe?"

Canavan's eyes glinted.

"When I wore it," he replied steadily, "nobody ever accused me of being afraid of my own shadow."

"N-o, but they accused you of other things, didn't they?"

"All right, Embree. We know what we think of each other. Now I'll add this much and you guide yourself accordingly. You stay the hell outta my way, or I'll shove that star down your throat. That clear?"

The sheriff didn't answer. Canavan shouldered him out of his way and marched off. Aggie, standing in front of a hitch rail a couple of doors beyond the lunchroom, looked up and when he approached and, recognizing him, whinnied, back away from the rail and plodded along after him.

5

TUCK WELLS, tying a clean white apron around his middle, was standing on the veranda looking down-street when Canavan crossed and came up the steps to the saloon. Tuck greeted him with a grin and his usual half-salute, turned and led the way inside. From the napkin-covered shelf behind the bar he selected a half-filled bottle of whiskey, uncorked it and placed it on the bar in front of Canavan and followed it with a glass.

"Had yourself a kinda busy morning, didn't you?"

Canavan grunted an indistinct response and poured a drink for himself.

"In case you don't know it," Wells went on as Canavan raised the glass to his lips, "you got Doak Potter, Nye's foreman."

"That so?"

"He's the one layin' in the gutter."

Canavan swallowed his drink.

"Gotta hand it to you, partner," Wells continued as Canavan put down the glass. "Nobody else around these parts has ever had the guts to stand up to Coley Nye. Everybody's always kowtowed to him. It's been that way for so long, it's become what you might call a habit. And it's kinda got him spoiled. Go on, partner. Help yourself. It's on the house, so fill 'er up again."

"Thanks," Canavan acknowledged. "But one'll do me fine for now."

Wells did not press his invitation.

"Now with Coley only able to use one hand, the left one at that, he has to leave things he'd be the one to do to somebody else. And so far," Wells grinned again, "the somebody elses he's picked haven't got very far with you according to what I've heard tell. So when he hears what happened this morning, he'll have a fit. What d'you suppose will happen now, partner? I mean, with those nesters movin' in on us?"

Canavan looked at him blankly.

"Mean you don't know about them? About those six families that hit town late last night?"

"Nope."

"They came in long about midnight. The sheriff talked to the leader, and after a while they pulled out. Headed north, I understand."

"What's out that way?"

"Trouble, if they decide to stay put there," Wells replied. "A bunch of small spreads, with two-, three-man crews. And you know something? Those two-bit outfits can be a heap nastier when it comes to nesters than the big ones. So I'm expecting trouble, and lots of it too. Say, didn't I see you talkin' to Embree down the street a while ago? Didn't he tell you anything?"

Canavan shook his head.

"Guess he had other things on his mind," Tuck said. "Anyway, I told you, so now you know."

Canavan hitched up his pants, shifted his holster a bit as Wells watched.

"Thanks for the drink," he said as he walked to the door.

"Forget it," Tuck answered.

Canavan went down the steps to the walk. He glanced downstreet mechanically.

Little groups of men were still standing around the dead men. He could see Giffy in the middle of one group; he bulked up so much bigger than the other men around him. But there was no sign now of Embree, and for a moment Canavan wondered what had become of him. He forgot about the sheriff when Aggie pushed her head over the hitch rail and nuzzled him. He patted her and she whinnied happily. He lifted his gaze instinctively when he heard approaching hoofbeats. Molly Fisher with her young son sitting in front of her came down the street astride the family horse, a plodding, wearied and rather dejected looking animal. When they came abreast of him, Molly smiled at Canavan and he acknowledged with a grave lift of his hat. Johnny, suddenly spotting him, called to him and he smiled back at the boy and waved to him too. They trotted past him and he followed them with his eyes, saw them turn in to the rail in front of Shotten's place. He saw Molly climb down, reach up for Johnny and help him down. Together, with Molly holding the boy's hand, they

112

went into the general store. Canavan followed them downstreet. He was waiting for them in front of Shotten's when they emerged some minutes later. Johnny was clutching two small packages to his breast.

"Get what you wanted?" Canavan asked as they came together.

"Oh, yes," Molly responded.

"Good."

"That Mr. Shotten was rather grumpy at first," she related, "and I was expecting him to tell us to go elsewhere as he did before. But he happened to glance out once and he must have seen you because his attitude seemed to change after that and while he wasn't particularly talkative, he was friendly enough."

Canavan untied their horse, held the stirrup for Molly and helped her climb up into the saddle. Then he boosted Johnny up, helped him settle himself in front of his mother.

"Find you were out of something you forgot to have me get for you?" Canavan asked.

"Yes. Oh, incidentally, do you know we have neighbors now?"

"You mean those homesteaders who hit town last night?"

"Yes. They're a couple of miles north of us. It will be nice to have someone to visit with now. There are some children among them, too, children close enough to Johnny's age to provide him with companionship and playmates."

His eyes held on her, clung to her as though he were committing to memory every feature, every detail of her face. She blushed a little under his steady, almost embarrassing gaze. Now, all of a sudden, he knew what it was that was keeping him in Cuero. It wasn't what he had told the sheriff. He had thought he was telling Embree the truth; he hadn't realized then that there was a far better reason for his refusal to move on, and that the reason was Molly. He hadn't known it then. But he did now. He wanted her. Fisher wasn't the man for her. He wasn't good enough. He didn't appreciate her, didn't deserve her either. But he, Canavan, was her kind of man.

Hadn't she said as much? Admittedly, not right out, nor in so many words. But the meaning was there, all right; he had but to recall her words and read between the lines to know what she had been trying to tell him. Hadn't she told him that he could go far, that he was the kind of man who would fight for what he wanted and who would get it and who wouldn't let anyone take it away from him? Did any woman tell that to a man if she didn't want him in place of the one she had already?

He had to hold himself in check, had to keep his arms down when they arose to reach up for her. He wanted to tell her in a swift rush of eager words that she was not returning to Reuben Fisher, that he was taking her away with him. She would give him the purpose in life that he hadn't had for such a long time. For her he would be able to find himself again, to do the things he was capable of doing. It would be a new and a good life for him, and it would be for her too.

Fisher couldn't offer her anything that could compare with it. Life with him held no promise, nothing to look forward to, only drudgery, poverty and disappointment, and eventually, resignation to it. Fisher, a man who apparently lived within himself and who kept his thoughts to himself, would accept his lot. But every time he met Molly's eyes, he would see in them a look of resentment that would make him retreat even deeper into his shell, and he would become even less communicative than he was ordinarily. A wall would arise and build up between them, and they would find themselves having less and less to say to each other. Brooding and embittered, she would come to hate him, and he would come to hate her because of her unwillingness to accept their lot more gracefully. That was how they would close out their lives. Canavan was unwilling to believe that she would reject what life with him offered her, and return to Fisher.

Suddenly, though, he was aware of a strange and frightened look in Molly's eyes. She knew what he was thinking, he told himself, sensed it somehow as some women have a faculty for doing. But the frightened look worried him; it could mean only one thing, that she was afraid that if she stayed there even one minute longer that his desires would communicate themselves to her, and that she would yield to them. She wanted to, yet she was afraid. Flushing, she averted her eyes, and backed her horse away from the rail.

"Bye," she called as she wheeled the animal.

"Bye!" Johnny yelled.

Canavan didn't answer. Bitterly disappointed, he stood slope-shouldered, rooted to the spot. He watched them ride away, followed them with his eyes till they were out of sight. He was motionless for perhaps a minute longer, then he stirred, drew a deep breath, straightening up and squaring his shoulders at the same time. Now he could go. There was nothing to keep him in Cuero. Nye meant nothing to him; neither did anyone else. Nye could return to riding roughshod over everyone. It didn't matter one way or another to him. The Fishers and the other nesters would have to protect themselves as best they could; if they were driven off, it would be their misfortune, and of no interest to him.

He strode into Shotten's, bought some bacon, flour and coffee, carried his purchases across the street to the waiting mare and stuffed them into his saddlebags. He flung a last bitter-eyed look at the town, climbed up on Aggie's back, wheeled her away from the rail, and rode off. Cuero, he told himself grimly as he reached the corner and left the town behind him, would never see him again. And if he never heard of Cuero again, it would be all right with him. Aggie, eager to run and given her head, broke into a swift gallop. A mile or two from town, Canavan spied an oncoming horseman and he pulled the drumming mare off the middle of the road. Then minutes later, the townward bound horseman and he came together. The oncoming rider was the sheriff. Canavan slowed the mare and pulled her back into the middle of the road, blocking Embree's way. The two men halted their mounts. Embree eyed Canavan rather wonderingly.

"Got something to tell you, Embree,"

Canavan announced, easing himself in the saddle.

Aggie, eager to go on, pawed the ground impatiently, and Canavan had to pull back sharply on the reins to make her stand still.

"Only thing I want to hear from you is that you're leaving Cuero," the sheriff answered grumpily.

"That's what I want to tell you."

Embree's head jerked.

"Huh? You mean that? You mean you're finally leaving Cuero?"

"That's right. I've had enough of Cuero, fact is, too much, and I think Cuero's had enough of me. So I'm heading out."

"That doesn't mean you won't think different about it after a while and come back again, does it?"

"I won't be back."

They sat facing each other in silence. It was the sheriff who broke it.

"Sorry we had words, Canavan," he said.

"Forget it."

"Where are you heading for?"

"A long way from here. California."

Embree nodded.

"Good idea, although I think I suggested that to you just the other day. New country, new faces, people who don't know any more about you than you do about them, a fresh new start . . ."

"I've been there before, so I know what California's like and what it has to offer."

"Oh," Embree said.

There was another span of silence. This time, though, it was a somewhat awkward silence as each man appeared to be waiting for the other to initiate their parting. Since neither man did anything to bring it about, it might have gone on indefinitely if it hadn't been for Aggie. Unable to bridle her impatience any longer, she pawed the ground, snorted and tossed her head, and Canavan, finally forced to do something about it, straightened up and said:

"Well, Embree, that's it. Guess I might as well get going."

"Looks like that mare of yours is kinda anxious to get going too," the sheriff commented.

They backed away from each other,

Embree's horse moving obediently, Aggie prancing light-footedly.

"So long," Canavan said.

"So long, Canavan," the sheriff responded, "and good luck."

Canavan acknowledged with a wave of his hand. That was their parting. There was no handshake because neither man offered. They loped away, and soon each was out of sight of the other. Half a mile farther, when Canavan emerged from a tree-lined stretch of roadway, he lifted his eyes. There wasn't a single cloud in the bright sky, not even the tiniest puff. The fenced-off fields on both sides of the road began to slope downward from it and, after a gentle drop of some two or three feet, leveled off again in a tableland that spread away in every direction as far as Canavan could see. It was solidly green, with tiny splashes here and there of brown, to break the monotony of the green. Here and there too were tiny rises to give the range a slightly humpbacked appearance, making it look as though some giant foot had scuffed up the greenish carpet while striding across it. But it was a peaceful scene that unfolded itself before Canavan, with no movement of any kind to mar its tranquility. The pleasant smell that lifted from the lush grass blended with the perfumed fragrance that came from the clusters of vividly hued wild flowers that studded the range, and came sweeping over the land and broke over Canavan, bathing him with its richness.

A mile slipped away behind Canavan, then another. Suddenly the cut-through that led to the Fisher place was just ahead of him. He slowed the mare as he neared it, stopped her altogether when he came up to it and stood up in the stirrups, and with eager eyes probed the homestead that lay about a quarter of a mile inland from the road. There was no one about, not even young Johnny. Canavan held his gaze on the house, hoping that the door would open and that Molly would come out so that he might have one last look at her. But it didn't open, and after a while when he realized the futility of waiting any longer he sank down in the saddle, disappointment showing in his face and in his rounded shoulders.

Aggie turned her head and looked at him. He met her eyes and promptly frowned.

"Well?" he demanded. "What are you waiting for?"

The mare's head jerked around. She trotted away. After a bit she quickened her pace.

It was noon and they were cutting across the range in a northward direction when they came to a tree-shaded brook. Aggie, whinnying, broke stride and pulled up. Canavan grunted and swung down from her, patted her on the backside, and she plodded down the bank. Squatting on his haunches at the top of it and chewing on a blade of grass, he watched her poke her nose into the gurgling water and begin to drink. When he thought she had had enough, he arose and called:

"All right, Aggie. Let's go."

She pretended she hadn't heard him. He stalked down the bank and backed her away from the water, and she protested loudly.

"That's enough outta you," he told her. "What d'you wanna do, drink up the whole brook? You would, all right, if I'd let you. How many times do I have to tell you that too much water's not good for you?"

She whinnied and tried to nuzzle him, but he would have none of her and he pushed her head away, climbed up on her and rode her up the bank. But then, topping it, he stopped her, debated something with himself, twisted around and looked down at the water, wheeled her and rode down again. She didn't understand, and when he dismounted she turned questioning eyes on him. It was only when he opened one of his saddlebags and hauled out a small, fire-scorched and battered-looking coffeepot that she understood. While he set about preparing his coffee, she plodded away, found a cropping of fresh young grass and began to munch it.

Canavan drank his coffee while sitting under a tree that arched out protectively over the water. And when he finished, he sat hunched over, staring moodily over the shadowy brook. It was only when Aggie returned to his side and nudged him that he got up on his feet. Minutes later, they topped the bank for the second time, and wheeling northward again went on their way. Aggie set her own pace, trotting, loping when the fancy moved her, and trotting again, but Canavan did not interfere with her. He was satisfied to let her go on as she pleased. The sun was at its hottest then, a brassy, flame-tinged mass that seemed to be spewing fire and wilting heat in every direction. Aggie's body was sweat-matted. Canavan's shirt was wet and it clung to him. He wondered once if it wouldn't have been wiser of them if they had stayed at the brook under the cooling shade of the overhanging trees till the heat slackened off. Perhaps if they hadn't been so far from the brook at that particular moment, he might have been tempted to return to it.

Twice they passed small herds of grazing cattle. Each time, as they neared the bunched-together steers, they were greeted by a deep-throated and chorused lowing; but once they were past them, the cattle resumed their grass munching.

Then suddenly, when Canavan happened to be lazying in the saddle, Aggie whinnied and slowed herself to a mere walk, and Canavan looked up. Coming toward them at an awkward and lumbering lope was a riderless horse. The stirrups of his empty saddle swung a little wildly and thumped against his sides and belly. They came together shortly, the riderless animal and Aggie; when the former showed too much interest in the mare and moved just a little too close to her, she snorted threateningly, and the warned-off animal hastily backed away.

There was no brand on him, Canavan noticed. He belonged to a nester, Canavan decided. Homesteaders, slow to adopt western customs and practices, never branded their horses, not even their few heads of stock. A nester had once told him that he considered burning a brand in the hide of an animal an unnecessary cruelty and refused to have anything to do with such a barbaric practice. Nor did the loss of his only horse persuade him to safeguard his property when he found it necessary to buy another horse. Of course, the nester's second horse was also run off, and the man who stole him brazenly branded him with his own initials and defied the complaining nester to prove his ownership of the stolen animal.

"Wonder what he's doing around here?" Canavan mused. "If one of those two-bit cattlemen that that bartender was talking about get his hands on him, the nester will never see him again."

They went on again shortly. The nester horse loped after them. Aggie watched him alertly, and whenever it appeared that he was about to overtake her, she lengthened her stride and quickly widened the gap between them. Twice Canavan shooed off the pursuing horse; the animal simply circled around, and the moment Canavan settled himself the pursuit was on again. Aggie refused to allow the heat to deter her; she had broken into a swift gallop, and doggedly she maintained the killing pace. Then all of a sudden, when Canavan was sweeping the range with his hand-shaded eyes, seeking a sign of the thrown rider, he spotted something in the thick grass some distance away that made him swerve

Aggie and send her bounding toward it.

As they neared the spot, there was a cry, and a tow-headed, sobbing boy arose. When he saw Canavan coming toward him, he ran to meet him. Skidding up to him in a stiff-legged slide, Aggie came to a panting halt. Canavan flung himself off the mare's back and caught the sobbing boy in his arms, and dropped to his knees with him. Johnny flung his sturdy little arms around Canavan's neck and clung to him, his body heaving as his frightened crying continued.

"All right, Johnny," Canavan told him. "You're all right now. I've got you. So don't cry."

The boy's sobbing tapered off shortly, and when it finally ceased, Canavan produced his bandana and, holding him off, wiped his eyes for him, made him blow his nose too. There was a dirt smudge on one cheek and still another on the very tip of his nose, and Canavan carefully removed them. And when he got up on his feet with the boy again in his arms, and turned with him, Aggie plodded forward and nuzzled Johnny. He reached out and patted her and she whinnied softly and sought to nuzzle him again, only to have Canavan push her head away and lift the boy into the saddle. Canavan climbed up behind him and hooked a protective arm around him and said lightly:

"Don't want to lose you now that I've just found you."

There was no need for him to ask the boy what had happened. Johnny had managed somehow to get up on the Fisher horse, and the animal had simply run off with him.

"I hit him to make him go faster," he heard Johnny say. "Then I tried to stop him, to make him turn around. But he wouldn't. He went even faster. And I got frightened."

"Uh-huh. And when you saw your chance you jumped off."

"Yes," Johnny acknowledged. "I wanted to go home."

"Good thing for you the grass 'round here is thick and cushioned your fall. Otherwise you might have broken your neck."

"Gee," the boy said. "That . . . that would have been awful."

"I'm afraid it would," Canavan said gravely.

The Fisher horse trotted up as they wheeled in the direction of the homestead and loped after them. Aggie wanted to run, but Canavan held her down. She tossed her head and snorted angrily and pranced a bit; when Canavan had had enough of her antics, he whacked her an openhanded slap on the rump that made her stop short and look around at him indignantly. Calmly he stared back at her.

"Well?" he wanted to know, and Johnny giggled.

Aggie's head jerked around. This time, though, she behaved herself and loped over the grass evenly.

They were probably a mile from the homestead when Johnny suddenly sat upright and pointed excitedly. Canavan, raising up, followed the boy's pointing finger with his eyes and saw a half-walking, half-running figure coming toward them. It was Molly. Johnny yelled to her and his voice carried across the range; she faltered to a stumbling, exhausted stop, and raising her head, stared hard. Johnny yelled again. She lurched forward, and forgetting her weariness, came flying over the grass. Canavan halted the mare and swung down with Johnny, sent him scurrying away with an affectionate pat on the backside, and watched him run into his mother's arms. She held him tight, rocked with him, and cried a little. She was dabbing at her eyes with a balled-up handkerchief when Canavan, with Aggie plodding along at his heels, came up to her.

"I'm beginning to think that fate brought you to Cuero for just one purpose," she began gravely. "To have you on hand whenever we need help, and it looks as though we need it regularly. Thanks so much, Canavan. Thanks so very much."

"Don't thank me," he responded. "I didn't do anything, and that's a fact. I just happened to be passing by when Johnny popped up, and all I did was boost him up in front of me, and well, here he is."

"H'm," she said, and both her tone and

her expression indicated that she wasn't overly impressed by his attempt to minimize the part he had played in returning Johnny. "When we returned from town," she related, "he pleaded with me to let him ride our horse around in front of the barn as you had let him ride yours. I went on to the house to put away the things I'd bought from Mr Shotten. I don't think it took me more than a minute or two. But when I came out, Johnny was gone."

"Gave you quite a scare, huh?"

"Yes. You have no idea what awful thoughts came to me. I was sure he'd been stolen, kidnapped, by one of the cattlemen. I . . . I got hysterical. I ran all the way to where Reuben was working and told him. I never saw him so enraged. It was my fault, he told me, and if anything happened to Johnny, he would never forgive me."

Canavan made no comment.

"Reuben hurried off to get the other homesteaders," she continued, "to help him search for Johnny."

"Uh-huh."

"They're some four miles from our

place. Since Reuben was on foot, I don't suppose he's gotten to them yet."

"Maybe I oughta ride after him and tell him Johnny's home," Canavan suggested.

"Oh, would you, Canavan?"

The Fisher horse had halted a short distance away. He looked up when he saw Canavan striding toward him; to Canavan's surprise, he stood meekly and offered no resistance when Canavan took him by the bit and led him back to where Molly and Johnny were waiting. The horse sought to nuzzle the boy; indignantly Johnny backed off from him. Canavan held the stirrup for Molly, helped her mount, and when she was settled in the saddle with her skirts tucked in under her legs, he lifted Johnny and sat him down in front of her, and passed her the reins.

Their eyes met and held. Molly flushed a little under his steady gaze. When the flush began to deepen, she jerked the reins and rode away. Canavan swung up on Aggie's back, wheeled her and drummed northward. After he had covered about a mile, he slanted northeastwardly. Half a mile farther he spied a trotting figure some hundred yards ahead of him. He cupped one hand around his mouth and yelled, and Reuben Fisher stumbled to an awkward stop and looked back. Canavan motioned to him to wait, whacked Aggie and sent her bounding away. Minutes later Canavan was pulling up at Fisher's side. The homesteader, chest heaving and wheezing, and exhausted-looking, lifted his eyes to him questioningly.

"He's home, Fisher," Canavan told him. Relief showed plainly in the homesteader's face.

"He . . . he's all right?"

"Yeah, sure."

"That boy," Fisher said with a shake of his head. He took out a bandana and mopped his sweaty face. "I'll have to do something about him."

"All he needs is a little companionship," Canavan said quietly. "His father's more than anybody else's. Now how about me giving you a ride back? You look kinda beat and it's a mile or so back to your place. So how about it?"

He kicked his foot free of the stirrup, reached down for Fisher and helped the homesteader swing up behind him.

6

AGGIE rounded the house at a trot and pulled up in front of it. Raising her head, she snorted loudly, as though she were summoning someone. Her head jerked in surprise when there was an almost immediate response; when the door opened and Molly came out, Aggie was a little startled, and she took a step backward instinctively, tilted her head and levelled an oblique look at Molly.

"Oh," Molly said when she saw her husband. Without looking at Canavan, she said: "You overtook him."

Fisher climbed down.

"Canavan says the boy's all right," he said to his wife.

"Yes," she answered. "It was a frightening experience for him, and while he appears to have gotten over it, I don't think he has completely. I hope you aren't going to punish him, Reuben."

"No," Fisher told her. "Of course not."

She looked relieved. The grimness in her face went out of it, and the tightening around her mouth eased.

"He's inside Reuben, if you want to talk to him. I think you should."

Fisher nodded, stepped around her and went into the house. As the door closed behind him, Molly raised her eyes to Canavan.

"Aren't you going to get down?" she asked.

"N-o, I don't think so," he replied. "I think it'll be better if I get going again."

She didn't say anything, made no detaining gesture. He wheeled Aggie. But then there was a not-too-distant rumble of wagon wheels; the thin creak of sweat-stiffened harness and the plod of horses' hoofs reached them, and Canavan pulled up abruptly and shot a questioning look at Molly over his shoulder. She followed him wonderingly, a little apprehensively too, to the side of the house, and ranged her gaze after his. From a northward direction came a strung-out line of swaying, cumbersome wagons, canvas-topped prairie schooners, lurching from side to side because they were top-heavy. They heard the front door open again but they did not take their eyes from the oncoming wagons. There were quick bootsteps behind them and Reuben Fisher came to his wife's side, took a step past her and peered hard at the lumbering schooners.

The driver of the first wagon spied him and waved, and Fisher said:

"Looks like the Wiggenses in the lead wagon." He took another look. "Yes, it is the Wiggenses. You remember them, don't you Molly? The people who lost their daughter when they were coming through the mountains and a snowslide hit them?"

"Yes," Molly said simply. "I remember them."

Canavan couldn't tell from her tone whether she liked them or not. She probably didn't, he told himself, or she would have shown more interest, given some outward sign of pleasure at seeing them again.

"Now what do you suppose has happened to them?"

The answer was all too obvious, and Canavan was glad the question hadn't been directed at him. His reply might have been a little too curt. He noticed, and was glad too, that Molly made no attempt to answer. He glanced at Fisher and asked himself: He have to ask a question like that? Can't he figure out for himself what must've happened? Does he have to be told that those nesters must've been driven off? He shook his head sadly. It hurt him to think of a woman like Molly being tied to a man like Reuben Fisher.

He shifted his eyes, held them again on the approaching wagons. There was a bonneted woman riding on the high, wide seat with Wiggens. He couldn't see much of her face, only her mouth and her chin, because the bonnet shaded the rest of it. But he could see her clasped hands in her lap. There was something tragic and pathetic about them that held his eyes. There was resignation and hopelessness in them, in the way she held them, and he felt sorry for her. Wiggens, he told himself grimly, was probably another Reuben Fisher, as unequal to what confronted him as Fisher was. If all the homesteaders were like him, then there was no place for them in Texas.

"Oughta be somebody with authority to keep these people from coming out here," he thought to himself. "To make them stay where they belong because it's a cinch they don't belong out here. They haven't got what it takes, the belly for it, the guts to fight for what they want. The cattlemen know it and they take advantage of it, and ride roughshod over them. So the best they can hope to get out've risking their lives crossin' the mountains and the prairie is the worst of it. The lucky ones, the way I see it, are those who don't make it."

Craning his neck, Canavan counted five more wagons strung out behind Wiggens'. As the train forged nearer the house, Fisher strode off to meet it. They came together shortly, Fisher and the Wiggenses, and the train ground to a halt. Mrs. Wiggens sat motionlessly, but her husband, leaning down from his perch, talked briefly with Fisher. Then the latter stepped back, squared around and marched ahead of the train. Canavan backed Aggie out of the way as the first wagon came trundling houseward. Molly moved back too. With Fisher leading the way, the wagons rolled past the house and pulled up in front of the barn in a solid line. Canavan heard handbrakes grate and rasp as they were yanked back. Presently men and women began to climb down from the wagons. They crowded around Fisher, and listened attentively to what he said to them.

"They seem to look up to Reuben, don't they?" Canavan remarked.

"Yes," Molly replied. "Probably that's why he's so glad to see them." Then she added: "In all fairness to him, they know he was a schoolteacher back home, and they have respect for him. Your Texans don't, and he feels it keenly."

"I can understand that, Reuben's making the most of it while he's got the chance. And I can't say that I hate him or blame him for it either."

"Molly!"

It was Fisher calling, turned away for the moment from his listeners.

"Y-es, Reuben?"

"Put on some coffee!"

He turned around again, and went on talking with the other homesteaders. Molly murmured an "Excuse me, please" to Canavan and went into the house. Now Fisher and the others were coming up from the barn. As they neared the house some of the homesteaders looked at Canavan; Fisher was among those who didn't. A couple of them trooped inside after Fisher; the others halted and idled outside. One of them, Canavan noticed, a comely young woman with a shawl draped loosely around her shoulders, stood a little apart from the others and looked at him rather interestedly. She sauntered about in what appeared to be an aimless circle that brought her gradually closer and closer to where Canavan was quietly sitting Aggie. Then when she was about four or five feet from him, she stopped and looked up at him, smiled and said:

"Hello."

He murmured an acknowledgment and touched the brim of his hat.

She dimpled and said:

"You aren't one of those awful cattle-men, are you?"

"No."

"Live around here?"

"Just visiting, you might say."

"Oh?"

She waited, apparently expecting him to tell her more. When he didn't, she asked:

"Your family with you?"

"Haven't any."

"Oh," she said again. "I guess that gives us something in common then. I haven't anyone either."

"Mean you came out here all by yourself?"

"My husband died shortly after we started out. Since there wasn't anything to return to," she shrugged. "I went on."

"Quite a trip to make by yourself."

She smiled deeply.

"I came through the mountains and over the desert without anything happening to me. That's more than I can say for most of the others in the party, even the men. What's your name?"

"Canavan."

"That's Irish, isn't it?"

"That's right," he said gravely.

"I'm Doreen Gregg. Are you a friend of the Fishers?"

He smiled and answered:

"I like to think so."

"What do you do?"

"Oh, I do a lot of things." He corrected himself. "Leastways, I *can* do a lot o' things. But I'm not doing anything now 'cept heading for California."

"Really?" Her eyes were bright and wide, and filled with eagerness and excitement. "I've heard it's wonderful country out there."

"It is," he told her.

"You mean you've been there already? That this won't be the first time for you?"

"I was there about a year an' a half ago."

"I wish I were going out there," she said wistfully.

"You've come this far by yourself," he said. "No reason why you can't make it the rest of the way."

"I'd go in a minute if there was someone else going along." She flushed a little and hastily added: "I mean if there was a party of people going and they invited me to join them."

"When you get to town, ask around, let people know that you're interested in getting to California, and you're liable to find others with the same idea just waiting for somebody to get them together and . . ."

"Are you . . . going alone?"

"That's right."

Her hands were on her hips now, her shoulders squared back. Her breasts were thrust forward, and seemed to be straining for freedom against the restricting bodice of her dress. Her lips were parted, moist and inviting, her eyes bold and challenging. Someone came out of the house and came toward them. Quickly the Gregg woman drew her shawl closer around her, criss-crossing the ends of it over her breasts. Molly stopped within a couple of feet of her. There was an angry flush in her cheeks, Canavan noticed.

"Coffee's ready," she announced, rather

stiffly he thought, addressing herself to Doreen.

Doreen gave her a smile.

"Oh, thank you," she said graciously.

Molly turned on her heel and stalked away. Doreen raised her eyes to Canavan, arched her brows, and said:

"I don't think she approves of me."

There was a sudden cry, and every head turned. A woman who had returned to her wagon, and whose left hand was curled around the top of the high front wheel preparatory to pulling herself up, pointed excitedly in the same direction in which the train had come.

"Look!" she shrilled. "They're coming here now!"

Canavan straightened up. In the distance he could hear the rhythmic, drumming beat of horses' hoofs. The beat swelled and came steadily closer and closer. Canavan glanced at the homesteaders who were standing about in front of the house. There were grim faces here and there, but there were frightened ones too, and they were in the majority. The door was flung open and

146

Reuben Fisher burst out, and skidded to a stop. Five horsemen, strung out in single file, whirled past the house and pulled up and wheeled around and rode back to it. The first man, a lean, greying man who appeared to be the leader of the band, sat back in his saddle while his winded, heaving horse bowed his head and, standing slightly spread-legged, blew himself. The other horseman formed a half-circle behind him and exchanged muttered side remarks with each other, and when they looked at the homesteaders Canavan could see the taunt in their eyes and the scornful twist to their lips.

"All right, you people," their leader began curtly. He had thin lips and a coldness in his voice.

"They're dirt under his feet," Canavan murmured to himself.

"Get back to your wagons," the cold voice continued, "and get rolling. And don't stop till you're across the county line. You," he said, pointing to Fisher. "Get your gear and clear outta here. I'll give you exactly five minutes to get your stuff outta there," and he indicated the house with a nod. "What's still in there after that goes up with the house. It's nothing but an eyesore and we're getting rid of it. Now get moving."

Canavan shot a look at Fisher. The homesteader's face was a chalky white, and twin, matching red balls in his cheeks burned against the stark whiteness. Now, Canavan told himself, the others who looked to Reuben for leadership would get a close-up view of him when he was called upon to take a firm stand.

"Well?" the lean man demanded impatiently. When Fisher did not move, he said simply: "All right, Fisher. If that's the way you want it." He turned his head. "Carly, I think he's gonna need some help gettin' himself started. Wanna see what you can do for him?"

A rather husky man who was sitting his horse almost directly behind him, grinned evilly and swung down, hitched up his levis and said:

"A hefty boot in the pants oughta do the trick for him, Boss."

He gave his levis another hitching up and started for Fisher. He was thick-legged and pigeon-toed, and he lumbered rather than walked. He was within a couple of strides of the homesteader when a gun roared suddenly, frighteningly, and a bullet plowed dirt squarely in front of Carly and spewed it over his boots and pants legs. He stopped instantly. Slowly his head turned. When his angry eyes found Canavan, he glared at him.

"Get back to your horse," Canavan ordered, gesturing with his gun. "Go on now. Back, I said." Slowly, reluctantly, the glowering Carly obeyed, backing off only because the gun that was holding on him seemed to gape at him with an ever-widening, menacing mouth. "You, Mister," he heard Canavan say, and he lifted his eyes to the greying man. "You own this property?"

"What business is it of yours?"

"I'm makin' it my business," he heard Canavan answer, and his gaze shifted to him mechanically, "and you can make anything you like out of that. This is range

149

land, free and open to anyone who wants to register it and work it. You'd better tell that maverick back of you, the one in the blue shirt, to keep his hands away from his gun, or I'll drill a hole right smack through the middle of him."

"Sit, Deac," the lean leader of the band said over his shoulder, and the man whose inching hand had caught Canavan's eye sat back, brought up his arms and folded them over his chest. Carly hoisted himself up on his horse's back and settled himself in the saddle. His eyes followed his mates', focused with theirs on Canavan who stared back stonily, unimpressed by the hard looks holding on him. Then the greying man said: "All right, boys. Let's go."

Their five horses were backed; however only four of them were wheeled away. Carly, a little unhappy-looking and still glowering at Canavan, hung back. But after a moment, apparently realizing the futility of it, he lashed his horse and sent him pounding away after the others. Canavan, holstering his gun, saw relief in the faces of most of the homesteaders, but not in Fisher's. The latter looked up at him and shook his head and Canavan asked:

"What's the matter?"

"I wish you hadn't done that, Canavan."

"Oh?"

"I suppose you think you did us a service, and that we should feel grateful to you. I'm sorry, but I don't feel that way at all. Frankly, I think you did us a disservice, that whatever chance we might have had of persuading that man Fleming to take a more reasonable attitude towards us is gone now."

"I see. You mean that if I hadn't interfered and if I had let you take another walloping, that Fleming might have felt sorry for you and maybe changed his mind about drivin' you folks off? Just how many wallopings d'you have to take before you get wise to the fact that you can't reason with or expect any sympathy out've a hard man who's gotten what he has the hard way, and who knows only one way, the hard, tough way, of dealing with others?" Canavan flung back at Fisher. "Are you blind, or just plain, downright stupid? Or is it thick-skulled, that you can't understand that kowtowing isn't gonna get you anywhere? Fisher, the best thing you can do, and this goes for your friends too, is pull outta here and head back to where you came from. Back to your farms, your stores, your books and your schoolhouse because that's where you belong and where you should've stayed."

"Now just a minute, Canavan . . ."

"Just a minute yourself! I'm not finished yet. Texas isn't the place for you people. This is a hard, rugged way of life, and the only ones who can hope to make a go of it out here are those who can stand on their own two feet. That lets you people out. You're soft and kowtowy and the people you're trying to move in on are hard and they won't give you an inch. Because they know you're scared to death of them and that you haven't got the guts to stand up to them, they ride rough-shod over you, trample you underfoot, run you off one place after another, and give you no peace, yet you think you can reason with them!"

There was no response from Fisher. The color that had drained out of his face, returned to it, flooding and flushing it.

"Maybe I shouldn't have horned in," Canavan went on. "Maybe I should have let you take another walloping. Maybe it would have brought you to your senses. On the other hand, maybe it wouldn't have. Chances are you'd still be stickin' to the idea that you can talk people who hate your guts into going easy with you. Well, from now on you can keep turning the other cheek and collecting all the wallopings you like. I won't be around to butt in on you and spoil things for you. I can't help feeling sorry for you though. But not half as sorry as I am for these people who seem to look up to you and who expect you to lead them, and for your family, because they'll have to suffer along with you when they shouldn't have to at all. That's it, Fisher. I've had my say. Now it's up to you. So long."

He nudged Aggie with his knees, and she raised her head and plodded away from the house. Doreen Gregg looked up and flashed a smile at Canavan, but he did not acknowledge it. He rode past her without a change in his grim expression. Aggie quickened her pace, broke into a trot, and drummed past the lined-up wagons and the barn behind them. Suddenly Canavan pulled up, twisted around and looked back. He thought he had seen a child's face peering out at him from behind the canvas drop curtain of one of the wagons. When he saw it again, he shook his head sadly, and rode on again. But instead of wheeling westward when he came to the end of the cut-through, he took the road that led back to Cuero.

It was night. Canavan, who had engaged a room in the local hotel, was in his room, lying in bed on the flat of his back with his clasped hands pillowing his head, his eyes staring moodily into the shadowy darkness around him. After a while he sat up, swung his legs over the side of the bed, groped for his boots, found them and pulled them on. He got up on his feet and stretched himself, rising up on his toes at the height of his stretch. His hat and gunbelt were on the chair next to the bed; he put on his hat, buckled on his gun and stamped out. A ceiling lamp, with a burned-down light burning in it that cast off a narrow circle of yellowish, eerie light directly below it and left the rest of the landing in shadows and darkness, guided his steps to the stairway at the far end of the floor. As he reached it and started down, a bulky figure started up the stairs. They stopped and looked at each other.

"Oh, hello, Embree," Canavan said.

The sheriff eyed him and frowned.

"Heard you'd come back and I was on my way up to see you," he said rather curtly. "And I thought we'd seen the last of you. No such luck though, huh? Mind telling me what brought you back?"

"Something came up," Canavan answered.

"Uh-huh. And you came back to take care of it. How long d'you figure it'll take you?"

"'Fraid I can't tell you that, Sheriff. It all depends."

155

"On what?"

"On the way things work out."

"That doesn't tell me anything."

"Well, when you go askin' questions that don't have any answers, leastways ready answers, what do you expect?"

"Do I have to tell you again that we haven't had anything 'cept trouble around here since you hit town?"

"Was that trouble any of my making?"

"The way I see it, yes," Embree retorted. "Fact is, every last bit of it too. If you hadda minded your own business, and if you hadn'ta horned in on things that didn't concern you . . ."

He didn't finish; Canavan didn't give him a chance to finish. He came down the stairs, shouldered the sheriff out of his way, forcing him back hard against the wall, and squeezed past him.

"I'm not finished with you yet, doggone it!" Embree sputtered.

Coming off the last step, Canavan halted again and looked up at him.

"That's where you're wrong, Sheriff," he said evenly. "We were finished with each other a long time ago, only you didn't have enough sense to know it."

He wheeled around and stalked out to the shadowy street, stood at the curb for a moment or two, then he crossed the street and went up the steps to the veranda and into the saloon. The place was deserted. Tuck Wells greeted him with a quick smile as he hunched over the bar about a dozen feet from the doorway, and asked:

"How's tricks, partner? Doing all right for yourself?"

"Oh, so-so," Canavan answered. "Where's all your trade tonight?"

"Middle of the week it's always slow."

"Oh!"

"What'll it be?"

"Beer."

"Coming up."

Wells looked out toward the darkened veranda, then he leaned over the bar.

"Have any more run-ins with Nye's outfit since that last one up the street?" he asked.

Canavan shook his head.

"See anything of his bunch?"

"Nope."

"Then what I heard must be right. Hear he's keeping his crew close to him. Guess he figures he's fooled around enough with you. Next time he goes after you, he aims to do the job right. No sending a lot o' saddle tramps out to do it." Tuck stole another look doorward, then he went on. "Understand his wrist wasn't as bad as it looked. Fact is, it's coming along fine now. Got himself a young doctor who seems to know his business and Coley swears by him. Another couple o' days and he's gonna let Coley use the wrist."

"Uh-huh."

"Then you're gonna have to watch yourself."

Canavan nodded and said:

"Thanks for the tip."

Wells grunted and turned away to the tap, served Canavan and sauntered off again.

Canavan was drinking his beer when he heard someone coming up the steps to the veranda. He levelled a glance doorward. A man with a heavy-legged, lumbering swagger in his walk came in. It was Carly. He gave no sign of recognition, simply stared at Canavan for a moment, then he walked up to the bar and leaned over it. Tuck was restacking some glasses on the shelf behind the bar.

"Be right with you, Carly," he said over his shoulder and Carly grunted.

Then there were more bootsteps outside, and presently two men appeared in the doorway. Canavan recognized them at once. One of them was Deac, the blue-shirted man with the inching gun hand; his companion was another Fleming hand, a thin man with a long neck, a jerking Adam's apple and twitching jaw muscles. Deac led the way inside. Meeting Canavan's eyes with a stony stare as he came abreast of him, he walked on to the far end of the bar and turned around there. The third man backed against the side wall opposite Canavan.

Glancing at Wells, Canavan saw a look of apprehension come into his eyes, and he said:

"It's all right, Wells. I've been braced before."

He put down his glass and eased himself around with his elbows thrust back and resting on the lip of the bar with his hands dangling, the right one a little lower than the left.

"Well?" he asked tauntingly. "Who's gonna start it? You, Carly? Or is that your job, Deac?"

He knew he had little to fear from Carly; he was clumsy in his movements, hence he would be awkward and slow in his draw.

The thin man didn't worry him either. His face was ashen colored, and his Adam's apple was jerking furiously.

"Scared to death," was Canavan's opinion after stealing a quick look at the man. "Wonder how they managed to talk him into this deal? He isn't gonna be any help to them. That's for sure."

Canavan turned his head slightly in Deac's direction. The man in the blue shirt would be the one to watch. He was tall and rangy, and doubtless quick with his hands. He would be the one to make the first move.

The next moment Deac confirmed it. His right arm jerked backward as he went for his gun. But Canavan was far faster. His gun was in his hand and levelling for a shot before Deac's gun muzzle cleared the thick lip of his holster. There was a thunderous blast of gunfire. It rocked the saloon, caromed off its walls. There was a slight pause, hardly more than a second or two, then there was a second blast. There was no more shooting after that.

When Tuck Wells dared raise his head and peer cautiously over the edge of the bar, only two men were still on their feet, Canavan, crouching a little, and the thin man. The latter, white-faced and bulgy-eyed and gulping, had thrown down his gun and stood facing Canavan with his hands held high. Wells raised up a little higher. Deac was sitting on the floor a step away from the bar, hunched over, with his arms folded and pressed against his stomach, and with his knees half drawn up. Blood surged over his hands and dropped between his legs. Tuck caught his breath and shot a quick look in Carly's direction. He stared a little, blinked and looked a second time, but the result was the same. There was no sign of Carly. He scurried out from behind the bar, stopped and looked down at the floor in front of it where Carly had been standing, spun around and ran to the doorway. A lurching, swaying figure that was poised over the top step held him wide-eyed and a little open-mouthed. When he thought that Carly was about to topple, he stepped out on the veranda and reached for him with one outflung hand. It was too late; his lunge was too short. Carly pitched out into space and struck the planked walk at the foot of the steps with a resounding crash. Quickly Tuck ran down the steps.

"Put your hands down," Canavan curtly instructed the thin man. "Stay where you are though till I decide what I'm gonna do with you."

He turned his back on the man deliberately, gulped down the rest of his beer, and pushed the empty, foam-ringed glass back on the bar. There were voices outside, excited and panting voices, and running, converging bootsteps. Then he heard them on the steps, on the veranda too. He didn't turn his head. Men came into the saloon; he heard them pass him, those who went to Deac's side, and he too looked in that direction. Deac had slumped over and now he lay motionless on the floor on his side. Canavan turned his head the other way when someone came up to him. It was the sheriff.

"Still at it, huh?" Embree demanded. There were other men behind the sheriff, in the doorway and on the veranda, and Canavan took notice of them but without interest. "Still adding to the notches on your gun."

Wells came into the saloon.

"It wasn't his doing, Sheriff," the bartender said. He was a little breathless. "Like I told you, they tried to brace him. Only he was too fast for them. He beat them to the draw."

"What difference does it make whose doing it was?" Embree demanded fiercely, suddenly whirling around on Tuck and startling him so that he hastily stepped back. "Killing is killing."

163

Wells had no answer for him. He turned away slowly, rounded the bar and took his place behind it. Canavan slapped a coin on the bar, hitched up his levis and strode doorward. Men gave way before him, opened a path for him, and he marched out. A handful of men were standing around Carly's body; they looked up when he came down the steps, but he passed them with a glance, cut across the street and went into the hotel. Minutes later he was back in his room, lamp-lit this time. Ridding himself of his hat and his gunbelt, he paced the floor, grinding his right fist into the palm of his left hand. He stopped and listened when he heard footsteps on the landing. They came up to his door. Then there was a knock on it.

"Yeah?" he called, half turning.

"Canavan?"

It was a woman's voice, one that he recognized at once, that made him go swiftly to the door and open it. Then Molly Fisher and he were looking at each other over the threshold.

7

STANDING just outside the door, with the hood of her cloak framing her face, standing in soft shadow and turned-down lamplight, she was the most desirable woman he had ever seen. She wasn't just pretty; she was lovely, even lovelier than he had thought. Daylight, he told himself, was not a fitting frame for such loveliness as hers; the glaring sunlight gave everything the same color tone. Night, shadow and lamplight were made for beauty, showed it off to its fullest advantage, gave it the soft, gentle setting that it needed and deserved. He was so hungry for her, it was all he could do to keep from reaching out for her, crushing her in his arms and tasting the rich goodness of her lips. There was a becoming flush in her cheeks, and it deepened a bit under his hungry eyes.

"Aren't you going to ask me in?" she asked shortly with a quiet little smile.

His head jerked at the sound of her voice. "Huh?" he asked. "Oh!"

He backed quickly with the door, opening it wide and holding it for her. She crossed the threshold, took another step inside the room so that he could shut the door. When she heard it close behind her, she turned to him, pushing down the hood and letting it hang between her shoulders. Her hands came up again. She touched her hair, fluffing it up the barest bit.

"I was afraid I'd be too late," she told him. "Afraid you'd be gone."

"I decided to stay over for another day. But how'd you know here to find me?"

"I didn't really." He had backed against the closed door. As he walked away from it, moving around her, she turned after him, following him with her eyes. He stopped when he came to the bedstead and backed against it and stood a little slope-shouldered, cross-legged too, with his arms folded over his chest. "I figured that if by some remote chance you hadn't yet left Cuero, then you'd have to have some place to spend the night. That meant the hotel.

There wasn't anyone downstairs at the desk. But the book on it was open and I looked at it, found your name and your room number, and came right up."

He took his hat and gunbelt from the chair and put them on the bureau, and brought the chair forward for her. She acknowledged with a murmured "Thank you" and seated herself in it, and sat back with her hands in her lap and her eyes lifted to him.

"Well, Molly?" he asked when he couldn't restrain himself any longer.

He had tried to put a lighthearted note in his voice to cover up his eagerness. His heart was thumping so wildly as he waited hopefully for her reply, he was sure she could hear it. Her answer had to be the one he wanted. It couldn't possibly be anything else. She wouldn't have come to him unless she had left Reuben.

"Will you do something for me, Canavan?"

He looked at her with surprise in his eyes. What kind of a question was that? What was the idea of it? If she had left

Reuben for him, as he was confident she had, why couldn't she come right out with it? Then the thought came to him that while she knew how he felt about her, that wasn't enough for her—that just reading it in his eyes wasn't enough assurance for her, that she might be waiting for him to tell her openly what he had never actually said to her, before she would feel free to tell him what he wanted to hear.

"Do you have to ask, Molly? Don't you know I'd do anything in the world for you?"

There it was. He had said it. Perhaps not the way she might have wanted it said. Still it was plain enough. She couldn't possibly want any more assurance than that.

"Will you . . . will you come back to us?"

He swallowed hard. She hadn't left Reuben after all. And all she wanted of him was a favor. The hurt he felt was reflected in his voice despite his efforts to conceal it from her.

"What's the idea?" he wanted to know, and his voice sounded gruff, even harsh, to his ears. He cleared his throat, unnecessarily and irritatingly, made a wry face and swallowed again, and muttered lamely: "Sorry. Something musta stuck in my throat."

"We want to prove to you and to everyone else that we aren't the weaklings we appear to be. We think we're quite capable of doing everything required of us. Even die if we have to. But we need someone strong, someone like you, Canavan, to get us started in the right direction."

"This your idea?"

She shook her head.

"Don't tell me it was Reuben's. I'd find it hard to believe. 'Specially after what happened today."

"Actually it was that Gregg woman who suggested it," she answered evenly, "and everyone approved the idea. It was decided that Reuben would go after you and ask you to return. But at the last minute. . . ."

"He lost his nerve, huh?"

"I was afraid you might not agree if he asked you . . ."

"So you offered to go in his place because

you knew I wouldn't turn you down. Right?"

She made no response. She averted her eyes, looked down at her hands, turned them over and over, studied and examined them critically.

"And I thought, leastways I hoped, you'd come to me for another reason. Guess I've been hoping for something I hadn't any right to hope for." He straightened up, walked to the window and stood there with his back to her. "I don't know, Molly. I don't know what to say. I'd like to do it. 'Course not because of the others, because they don't mean anything to me. But for you. But I'm crazy about you. Then to be near you every day and to have to keep my distance, wanting you so much that it hurts but not being able to do anything about it, it's asking a lot of me. An awful lot. And I don't know that I could go through with it."

"Would it be asking any more of you than it would of me?"

He turned slowly. He peered hard at her.

"Wait a minute now," he commanded.

"You mind repeating that? I wanna be sure I heard you right."

"Would it be asking any more of you than it would of me?"

"You mean you feel the same way about me that I do about you?"

"Oh, yes, Canavan! I thought you knew that."

They moved at the same time. He took a step toward her and stopped again, and she arose from her chair and started toward him with an outflung hand, only to stop too. They stood facing each other, about a foot apart, each wanting the other, yet denying themselves what they wanted.

"You never let on, Molly."

"Couldn't you see it in my eyes? I saw it in your eyes."

"What do we do?"

"What *can* we do?"

"Only one thing, Molly," he said quietly.

"You mean go 'way together."

"That's right."

"No, Canavan," she said with a shake of her head. "We can't do that. I know *I* can't.

I'm married to Reuben. I'm the mother of his child. They both need me, one as much as the other. If I deserted them, I'd never be able to live with myself. If I went away with you, as time went on I'd hate myself for what I had done, and I'd hate you too for having been a party to it."

"Yeah," he said heavily.

"So you see . . ."

"That it's one of those things that we can't do anything about? Oh, yeah . . . I can see that all right. See it as plain as day."

She raised the hood again, raised it around her head, drew her cloak a little closer around her and held it in place with one hand, turned and walked to the door. She halted with her free hand on the knob, looked back at him and said:

"Goodbye, Canavan."

He didn't answer. He tried to, but the words stuck in his throat and choked him. He heard the door close behind her, heard her light step briefly on the landing. He moved heavily to the window again and looked down into the darkened street. There was a buckboard drawn up at the curb in front of the hotel. Molly came out to it shortly, climbed up in it, and drove off. He stepped back from the window and sat down in the bed and slumped across it and lay there staring up at the cracked ceiling. But then he sat up again, got up on his feet, clapped on his hat and buckled on his gunbelt. He strode doorward, stopped just short of it, looked back and scowled. He had forgotten to turn out the light. He wheeled around, muttering darkly to himself, retraced his steps to the bureau, and with a twist of his wrist plunged the room in darkness. The door swung behind him and slammed as he stamped out. Minutes later he emerged from the hotel and strode downstreet to the stable at the far corner. Nearing it, he saw that the gate was locked. The proprietor of the stable lived above it. It took Canavan a couple of minutes to wake him, then he had to bridle his impatience and wait uncomplainingly till the grumbling stableman climbed into his pants and boots and trudged downstairs and admitted him.

Aggie was well rested and eager to run,

and Canavan did not hold her down once they had left Cuero behind them. The moment Canavan eased up on the reins, the fleet-footed mare bounded away. The miles vanished behind them in a drumming beat of flashing, pounding hoofs. They overtook Molly as she was wheeling off the road onto the cut-through. She pulled up at once when she heard Canavan call her name. He reined in alongside the buckboard.

"You came anyway," she said, a voice whose face he could barely make out in the darkness. "Even though there's nothing to look forward to."

"You knew I wouldn't turn you down, didn't you?"

"I didn't dare hope too much."

"If you can stick it out, I guess I can too. But it isn't going to be easy, Molly. You'd better make up your mind to that."

"Oh, I know it's going to be difficult," she assured him. "Maybe impossible at times. But I think we have the courage to go through with it. Now there's just one thing more that I want to say. I have to say it in fairness to you."

"All right. I'm listening."

"Canavan, if as time goes by you should begin to feel that you've made a mistake, that you shouldn't have returned here, that the future holds nothing for you here, just get up on your horse and go. Or if you should find that you've fallen in love with someone else. Don't come and tell me about it. I couldn't bear to hear you tell me about another woman. Just take her away with you. When I hear that you've gone, I'll understand, and I won't blame you."

"Look, Molly," he said. "If it's that Doreen Gregg woman you're thinking about, don't. Don't give her another thought. Y'hear? I've met others like her, some just as pretty as her, and some a heap prettier. But I didn't fall for any o' them and I don't aim to fall for her either."

"Johnny . . ."

It was the first time she had called him that.

"Yeah?"

"Will you kiss me, please?" she asked.

She lifted her face to him. He bent over her, cupped it in his big hands, felt a dampness on it and knew it was her tears. He whispered "Molly, Molly," felt tears course down her cheeks, and kissed her full on the mouth. She choked off a sob. Her hands came up and clung to his. When she drew them down, he moved back from her, squared back in the saddle. When the buckboard moved, its body and shaft creaking, he sat motionlessly, waited till it had pulled ahead of him. Then he rode after it and followed it and stopped again when Molly did, when they came abreast of the halted line of prairie schooners with the barn towering darkly and almost protectively behind and above them.

It was the following morning, exactly one minute after ten, when four horsemen loped into Cuero, and slowing their mounts to a trot, rode downstreet and pulled up in front of a store whose window bore the legend LAND OFFICE. They dismounted and tied up their horses at the hitch rail, mounted the curb and crossed the walk, and led by grim-faced cattleman Rick Fleming, trooped inside. Will Pierce, middle-aged, thin-haired and bespectacled, who was in charge of the office, looked up a little wonderingly from his desk when the four men entered.

"Fleming, Sturges, Booth and Kiley," he murmured to himself. "Far as I've ever heard tell, they never had any use for one another. Yet here they are together. Wonder what they're up to?"

He arose and sauntered forward to the railing, and as they came up to it he nodded and said:

"Morning."

"Morning, Will," the four cattlemen chorused.

"Nice day," Pierce said. When there was no response, only a grunt by Sturges that Pierce didn't try to interpret, he decided that the weather was not one of the matters that they had come to discuss with him. So he asked: "What can I do for you?"

"Will," Fleming began. "We're here to do some filing."

"You came to the right place to do it," Pierce answered. There was a table standing just beyond him, side flush with the railing, and on the table were a dozen or more curled-up maps. He reached for the one nearest him, unrolled it and studied it for a moment, nodded, and spreading it out on the railing said: "Picked out yours right off, Rick."

Fleming bent over it.

"There," he said after a brief study of the map. "Right there, Will." He used a broken-nailed finger to trace a line on it. "I'm filing on that section."

"I'm afraid not, Rick," Pierce said.

Fleming raised his eyes. "Huh? What d'you mean?"

"See the way it's been outlined in black ink? That means it's been filed on already. Matter o' fact, it was filed on just this morning. Right after I opened."

"Yeah? And who was it that filed on it?"

"Feller named Wiggens."

"Wiggens?" Fleming repeated. "Never heard of anybody named Wiggens 'round these parts before. You sure you got the name right?"

"I'm sure, Rick."

"But, damnation, Will, that's my land!" Fleming sputtered, his face suddenly flaming. "I've been grazin' my stock on it for years. Fact is, ever since I bought my spread from old man Schilling. And that'll be eleven years come this October. Then last year I even hired a couple of extra hands to help clear it."

Pierce's thin-bladed shoulders lifted in an unimpressed shrug.

"Then why didn't you file on it and make it yours legal?" he asked bluntly.

"You mean in spite of everything I've done, all the dough I've put out to make that section usable, I don't have any claim to it?"

"That's the general idea, Rick."

Sturges hitched up his belt and crowded up alongside of Fleming, disregarded the resentful look that Fleming flung at him, and said: "Will . . ."

Pierce shifted his eyes to him.

"Will, you know that section next to my property? Section eighteen, I think it is."

"Uh-huh."

"The piece with the line shack on it. I put

179

that thing up for my crew. You gonna tell me that's been filed on too?"

"That's right," Pierce replied calmly. "It was filed on this morning same's Rick's was. No more than five, ten minutes after."

Sturges' eyes were burning.

"And who did you say filed on it?"

"I didn't. But being that you've asked, I'll tell you. Feller named Fisher. Reuben Fisher."

"That's my land," Sturges said flatly, "and nobody's gonna take it from me."

"It's Fisher's now, according to law," Pierce told him evenly. "You try and take it back from him, and you'll find yourself with a tough United States Marshal to answer to."

Fleming snatched the map out of Pierce's hands and flung it away with an angry heave, spun around and stalked out. Sturges, scowling darkly, gave Pierce a hard look, turned on his heel, and stamped out too. Pierce shook his head. He turned his gaze on Booth and Kiley, and with another shake of his head, said:

"The way they took on, you'd think I

make the laws. Now if you fellers are here to file on land adjoining your spreads, you're outta luck. You're too late. It's been filed on already." But then Pierce lost his temper. "Doggone it! Ever since the homestead filing law came into being, I've been talkin' my fool head off, warning you fellers every chance I got, to file on your grazing lands. But did any of you pay any attention to me or to what I was telling you? Nope. Not a blamed one of you. And now that you find yourselves right smack up the creek, you wanna take it out on me. I get so blamed mad, I . . . I could spit!"

Sheriff Embree was alone in his office, filling the chair behind his desk to overflowing, hunched over the desk on his elbows and drumming on it with his fingers. When he heard approaching bootsteps outside, he sat back and waited. Rick Fleming, tight-mouthed and angry looking, came striding in.

"Oh, h'llo, Fleming," Embree said. "What . . . ?"

That was as far as he got. He stopped

because Sturges, with Booth and Kiley following at his heels, entered the office. He shuttled his gaze from one to the other, watched Booth and Kiley, two big, bulky men who rarely spoke for themselves and who preferred to have someone else do it for them, drift away to one of the side walls and stand there. Then he took his eyes from them, looked questioningly first at Fleming, then at Sturges.

"Well?" he asked finally. "What's this all about, and who's gonna tell me?"

Fleming, about midway between the door and Embree's desk, cleared his throat and said:

"It's this way, Sheriff. We ..."

"Hold it a minute," Sturges said, and Fleming, still annoyed with him, frowned. "You mind if we close the door, Embree?" He did not wait for an answer; he closed the door and backed against it, and said: "We don't want any outsiders bustin' in on us and getting an earful of something that doesn't concern them."

"H'm," Embree said.

"Go ahead, Fleming," Sturges said.

"Thanks," the greying cattleman said dryly. He stepped up to the desk. "Now look, Embree," he began. "We've just come from the Land Office. We've had us a session with Will Pierce, and now we're good an' sore. Nesters have filed on our grazing lands, and according to Pierce there isn't anything we can do about it. We think different. We think there is something we can do about it. But because we're law-abiding we don't want to start anything. We're putting it up to you. You're our man. We wanna know what you can do about it."

"Hate to disappoint you, Fleming," Embree replied. "And that goes for you others too. But you've come to the wrong place. Anything that has to do with land comes under the gover'ment and that's in Washington. So if you have any complaints, that's where you'll have to take them up. I'm a local lawman, a county law officer, and all I handle is local stuff."

"That's just the point, Embree. That's why we came to you," Sturges said. "Because what's got us so het up is local stuff."

"Right," Fleming said. "What's the gover'ment sitting on its tail in Washington, a thousand, fifteen hundred miles away, know what we're up against here in Cuero? But you're here, and if anybody knows what our problems are, you do. So we figured you'd be the one to set things straight for us. Now how about it?"

"What you fellers are asking me to do," the sheriff replied, "is buck the gover'ment."

"What gets me is this," Sturges said. "We pay the taxes the way the gover'ment tells us to, so what does the gover'ment do but turn around and pass a law that protects the outsiders who don't pay any taxes at all. How come the gover'ment is so all-fired anxious to protect them instead of us?"

No one offered an answer.

"Well, Embree?" Fleming asked.

"Y'know, I'm kinda surprised at you fellers," the sheriff began. "Seems to me, if I was a cattleman, and somebody moved on me, I'd know doggoned well what to do about it. And I wouldn't have to go looking for somebody to tell me what I could do either."

"That's fine," Sturges retorted. "But only as far as it goes. Trouble is you didn't go far enough. Supposing we were to, well, decide to handle this on our own, in our own way?"

"And?"

"What would you do about it?" Sturges asked boldly.

"Yeah," Fleming said, Sturges' boldness communicating itself to him. "What would you do about it?"

"Well, let's see now," the sheriff began in a rather musing tone. "I'd have to do something about it, wouldn't I, to make it look good? Wouldn't do, you know, for the law not to take notice of something happening in its own territory."

"Come on now, Embree," Sturges urged. "I asked you a straight out question. I want the same kind of answer."

"All right," the sheriff replied. "That's the kind you'll get. I've got a lot o' territory to cover, and I'm about due to ride out and kinda look things over. I do that two, three times a year, and it usually takes me a couple of weeks to make the circuit. Now if something was to happen around here while I'm away, I wouldn't know about it till I got back."

"Chances are that by that time," Embree continued, "the time I get back, everything would be peaceful again. The situation would be cleared up. The nesters would be gone and you fellers would be busy with your own problems. To make it look good though, soon's I heard there'd been trouble between you two, you cattlemen and the nesters, I'd go see about it. The nesters wouldn't be here so I wouldn't be able to get anything out've them. I'd have to go see what you fellers had to say about it. I expect I'd find the nesters had brought the trouble on themselves. They'd probably got a mite too big for their britches, a little too cocky for their own good, overstepped themselves, and you fellers had to hit back at them. I'd have made my investigation, and my report would say that as far as I could find, you fellers weren't to blame for what had happened, that it was forced on you by the nesters . . ."

"Yeah, but . . ."

"But what, doggone it!" Fleming sputtered, whirling around at Sturges. "You ask a man a question, and when he tries to answer, you don't let him finish."

When the offending Sturges flushed and averted his eyes, Embree continued:

"The marshal comes through here about every four months. He's due to hit Cuero in about eight, nine weeks from now. By the time he shows up here again, this business between you and the nesters will be cold turkey. So cold, I'll probably have forgotten about it by then. I'll tell him everything's quiet and peaceful around here, and he'll check off Cuero on his list and go on his way. Then the next time I see him, I'll suddenly remember what I forgot to tell him the time before. But by then it won't matter. It'll be a thing of the past."

"You're the damnedest feller to get a 'yes' or a 'no' answer out've," Sturges said a little grumpily. "Then you won't do anything if we decide to handle this by ourselves. Right?"

"He's just after telling you that, isn't

187

he?" Fleming flung at him over his shoulder.

"I'm asking him," Sturges retorted, red-faced. "Not you."

"You don't seem to understand him, so I'm answering for him," Fleming, flush-faced too, shot back.

"Now all I want," Embree said, disregarding the flare-up between Sturges and Fleming, "is to know a little in advance of when you fellers intend to go after the nesters. That'll give me and Giffy a head start getting out of town."

"Day's notice be enough for you?" Fleming asked.

"Yeah, sure," the sheriff replied. "I don't wanna know anything else though, how you figure to go about this, or anything. Only when. Now when you start makin' your plans, here's something you'll have to deal with first. The idea to file on your grazing lands wasn't something the nesters cooked up. Most of them never even heard of the homestead law. The idea came from somebody else, and before you can even hope to get at the nesters, you're gonna have to do something about him."

"Who d'you mean, Sheriff?" Fleming asked. "You talking about that Will Pierce?"

"He's talking about Canavan," Sturges said curtly.

"Oh, that big, redheaded feller," Fleming said. "Who in blazes is he anyway?"

"Canavan used to be a Ranger," Embree answered. "And he was a good one, too. One of the best they ever had. Got himself kicked out because he ran a little wild one day with his gun."

"Then the first thing we've got to do," Fleming said, "is get rid of him."

"Right," Embree said, nodding. "Only don't think it's gonna be easy, getting him that is, or that just anybody is gonna do the job for you. Coley Nye found that out, and you will too. 'Course there's this much to be said. No matter how good a man might be with a gun, he's still only one man. And if you're willing to lose a couple of hands, you can get Canavan. It all depends on if you're willing to pay the price."

"He's two up on me already," Fleming said grimly. "Deac and Carly."

"And he's about four up on Coley Nye," Sturges said. "And one of the four was Coley's kid brother."

"You fellers know what you're up against and you know what you've got to do," Embree said. "Now you've got to figure out how you're gonna go about doing it. Now why don't you go off somewhere, some place where it's nice and quiet, where you can talk and make plans? I've got things to do here and I'd kinda like to get at them. What d'you say?"

"Let's go," Sturges said.

He stepped back from the door, turned and opened it and went out. Booth and Kiley trooped out after them. Then Fleming trudged out. The door had barely closed behind Fleming when it was opened again, and Giffy came striding into the office. He looked questioningly at the sheriff.

"Hey," he said. "What was that all about? Oh, you want the door closed?"

"Huh?" Embree asked, lifting his eyes to him.

"What did they want here?" Giffy asked.

He closed the door and sauntered forward to the desk. The sheriff sat back in his chair.

"Giffy, what would you say if I told you we won't have to put up with Canavan much longer?"

"I'd say that's fine."

"Yes," Embree went on. "One of these days, and I don't think it will be long in coming either, we'll have seen the last of Canavan, and we'll have peace and quiet around here again."

Giffy gave him a searching look. There was a single, straight-backed chair standing against the wall; Giffy reached for it, brought it deskward, spun it around and straddled it, and thumbing his hat up from his forehead said:

"Suppose you quit talking in bunches and tell me what you and those others have cooked up for Mister Canavan? I'm what you might call an interested party, so let me in on it. Go on. I'm listening. So shoot."

8

IT was a little after five o'clock, and Will Pierce, preparing to close the office for the day, was drawing the faded and threadbare blind over the window. He looked a little surprised when he heard the door open; he stepped back from the window and looked toward the door, and when he saw Canavan enter, he grunted and trudged forward. They came together at the railing.

"I won't keep you but a minute, Pierce," Canavan said.

"That's all right," Pierce answered. He added with a wry little smile: "A few minutes more won't make any difference to me. I live alone and no one's waiting for me to get home. So if I'm a bit later than usual," his thin shoulders lifted in a shrug. "What can I do for you?"

"I've been wondering and I kinda hoped

you might be able to tell me what I'm curious about."

"If you've been wondering whether or not the cattlemen whose lands you people have filed on have been here already, they have. That is, four of them have been here. Fleming, Sturges, Booth and Kiley. The other two, Rawls and Weber, will probably be in tomorrow."

"That's part of what I was curious about."

"When they found that they were too late to file their own claims," Pierce continued, "they were quite put out about it. That's something else you were wondering about, isn't it, how they'd take it?"

Canavan grinned and nodded.

"When I told them there wasn't anything they could do about it, that the filings had been done completely within the law, they were pretty mad at me."

"I'm sorry about that," Canavan said quickly. "I didn't want to get you mixed up in this."

"Oh, I don't mind getting mixed up in it," Pierce assured him. "Fact is, I rather like the idea. Things get pretty dull around here and a touch of excitement is always a welcome change. I've known most of the people in Cuero a a long time, particularly the cattlemen. They're a rather smug bunch, and they've needed a taking down for some time now. You've given them that. You've jolted them like they've never been jolted before. But I'm afraid you and your friends are going to be in for it now. You haven't heard the last of this."

"No, don't suppose we have," Canavan admitted. "We'd be kinda surprised if the cattlemen gave up their grazing lands just like that. We expect them to fight to get them back. Only we're liable to give them the biggest surprise of their lives when they come after us. We're liable to give them as good as they give us."

"Incidentally," Pierce said, "when the four who were here stalked out, I saw them head straight for the sheriff's office."

"Oh, yeah? Wonder what they expected Embree to do for them? He isn't the smartest lawman I've ever met up with. Still I think he's got better sense than to try to buck the gover'ment, and that's what he'd be doing if he sided with the cattlemen in this and tried to defy the law."

Pierce offered no opinion.

"Still there's no telling with Embree," Canavan went on musingly. "No telling what he's liable to do."

"No," Pierce said bluntly. "There isn't."

"Take it you don't think any more of him than I do."

"I don't," Pierce answered evenly. "As far as I'm concerned he's still a storekeeper, and a rather unsuccessful one at that. And cast in the role of lawman, I don't think he's any better fitted for the job than he was for tending store. You'd better keep a sharp eye out for him as well as for the others, Mister."

It was later that evening, probably around nine, when Fleming topped the steps to the veranda and peered into the saloon. When he spied Sturges standing alone at the bar, hunched over it and toying with a half-drained whiskey glass, he sauntered inside, exchanged nods with Tuck Wells and halted at Sturges' side. The latter lifted his eyes and said:

"Oh. It's you, Fleming."

"You see Nye?"

"Yeah, sure, I saw him."

"And?"

Sturges shook his head.

"No deal, Fleming."

"You mean he won't go in on this with us?"

"Nope."

"What'd he have to say?"

"He isn't interested in the nesters. When they bother him, he'll go after them with his own outfit and he won't ask for help from anybody. Only one he wants is Canavan, and he's gonna get him too, if it's the last thing he does."

"Wish he was going after Canavan now," Fleming said.

"You and me both, because it would sure make things a lot easier for us. Without Canavan and his gun, those lousy nesters wouldn't stand a chance once we go after them. How'd you make out? See everybody you were supposed to see?"

"Yep," Fleming replied. "Saw every last one of them and got the same answer from all of them. They're with us, all right. Just waiting for us to say when."

"How many men will they let us have?"

"Gotta remember they're small outfits, Sturges."

"What's that got to do with it? They've all got hired hands working for them, haven't they?"

"Yeah," Fleming conceded. "Only most of them have just one hired hand, and only a couple of them have two men."

"So what?"

"So we can have a man here and another one there, maybe none at all from the next place because the feller who owns it can't afford a hired hand and he does his own work, and so on. All told though, I figure we can count on about twenty men."

"Twenty, huh?" Sturges repeated. "Add six including me from my outfit, Booth and Kiley, and we'll have twenty-eight."

"Hell, man, that's a regular army!"

"Wait a minute now, Fleming. Kinda forgot something."

"What's that?"

"You."

"Oh, I'll be along same as you."

"Yeah, but what about some of your hands?"

"With Deac and Carly gone, I've only got two left now."

"All right. Bring them along."

"Can't, Sturges. Dave Wiltse has been actin' up of late, so I won't ask anything of him. Soon's I can get somebody to fill in for him, I'm gonna pay him off. As for Tex Anders, he got himself banged up this afternoon. Probably got himself a couple o' busted ribs. His horse fell and threw him and rolled over on him."

"Then all told, counting you, we'll have twenty-nine. If that isn't enough to put an end to those nesters . . ."

"There are only what, six of them?" Fleming asked.

"Six in that one bunch and Fisher makes seven."

"And Canavan?"

198

"Eight," Sturges replied.

"Twenty-nine against eight," Fleming said. "Almost four of us to every one of them. We can't miss, Sturges."

"If we miss," Sturges said grimly, "we're done for. The nesters will drive us off the range instead of it being the other way around."

A man came up on the veranda, poked his head into the saloon, spotted Sturges, and hitching up his belt, strode down the bar to his side. When Fleming nudged him, Sturges turned around.

"Yeah, Waco?" Sturges asked. "Wanna see me?"

"For a minute, Boss," the man answered and glanced at Fleming.

Sturges noticed it and said:

"It's all right, Waco. Fleming's in on this with us, so you don't have to worry any about what you say in front of him."

Waco nodded.

"Saw that big red, that Canavan feller, coming out've the Land Office earlier this evening," he related in a low tone, "and it gave me an idea."

"Go on," Sturges said. "What was it?"

"Boss, supposing the records that Will Pierce keeps in his place were to, well, let's just say they upped and disappeared?" Waco paused and grinned, and his parted lips, easing back, revealed yellowish, tobacco-stained teeth. "What could those mangy nesters do then, and where would they stand without the records to back up their claims?"

"Why, doggone it, Waco," Sturges began excitedly. When Fleming clutched his arm and hissed at him "sh-sh. Take it easy, man. Keep your voice down," Sturges gave him a hard look and twisted away from him and turned again to Waco. But this time his voice was low and guarded when he said: "Waco, you're a smart feller. You've really come up with something. If those records were to, well, like you said, just up and disappear, those critters wouldn't have a leg to stand on. We could march right into Pierce and file on those lands for ourselves and nobody could stop us."

"That's the idea," Waco responded. "Boss, I've been planning to hit you up for more dough. If those records disappear, do I get it?"

"Tell you what, Waco," Sturges replied. "You bring them to me, and instead of the sixty a month you're pulling down now, you'll start drawing a foreman's pay. That's eighty bucks every month. How's that sound to you?"

Waco grinned broadly.

"Nice, awf'lly nice," he said. "Like music to my ears."

"Go earn it," Sturges said simply.

Waco hitched up his levis, nodded to Fleming, stepped around Sturges and strode out. Sturges looked obliquely at Fleming, and asked:

"Well? What have you got to say now?"

Fleming met his eyes and smiled a little sheepishly, shook his head and countered with:

"Why didn't we think of that?"

Apparently Sturges could not think of a fitting response. So he laughed and squared around to the bar and picked up his glass.

Waco's idea to steal the Land Office records

in order to thwart the nesters and nullify their claims had come to him a little belatedly. Canavan, anticipating such an attempt on the part of the cattlemen, had decided earlier that the records would be safer in his keeping than in Will Pierce's. While he was satisfied that the latter's sympathies were with the homesteaders, he felt that their rights needed the protection that Pierce couldn't very well furnish. Now, having circled the darkened town and coming up upon it from the rear, he reached the Land Office's backyard, found that like most of the others that he had passed, it was cluttered with discarded boxes and barrels. Carefully he threaded his way through the yard, and just as he was nearing the shadow-steeped building, a one-story affair that housed the office, he heard something in one of the alleys that flanked it. He flashed over the intervening space and flattened out against the building, seeking the screening safety of the shadows that it cast off and draped about itself. He heard the sound again, heard it a little clearer this time and recognized it as a bootstep, and listening to it, heard it coming steadily closer. Holding his gaze on the alley, he finally saw a stealthily moving figure round a corner of the building, hug the back wall and follow it doorward.

"Son-uva-gun," Canavan murmured to himself. "After the same thing, I'll bet, that I came for. Good thing for me I got here before he did."

Fortunately, Waco had no reason to suspect that someone else might be after the records too. So he sidled up to the door without so much as a glance about the yard. There was an almost protesting squeak from the door as the lock yielded to whatever it was that Waco used to force the door. The wood around the lock splintered, and the door opened and creaked back on its hinges and stopped. Waco glided over the threshold and disappeared from view. Canavan, with his hand on his gun butt, debated with himself, and finally agreed that he had no alternative but to wait for Waco to emerge.

"No sense in me going in there too," he thought to himself. "I'll just let this feller do the looking and find what he's after, and when he comes out, I'll jump him and take it away from him."

Long minutes, uneventful ones, passed. Finally, when his impatience got too much for him, Canavan inched up to the half-opened door and stole a look inside. He spotted a tiny flicker of light burning against the darkness. The light sputtered and suddenly went out, and he heard Waco curse. More minutes passed, about ten, he judged. He heard drawers and cabinet doors open and close, heard warped floor-boards creak underfoot as Waco moved about in his search. He heard Waco curse again, a little louder and a little angrier this time, heard a chair topple and crash, and he grinned inwardly. Then when Waco's boot-steps turned doorward again, Canavan beat a hasty retreat. He moved past his original position, flattened out against the building as before, and waited. Presently Waco came out of the office. He closed the door and stood for a moment in front of it, and when he finally trudged off, Canavan was satisfied that Waco had failed to find the records he had sought. He gloated inwardly as he watched Waco round the building and disappear.

Suddenly, though, his gloating stopped. A disturbing thought came to him. Suppose, he asked himself, that Pierce, just as aware as he was that the cattlemen might seek to steal his records, had removed them, taken them home with him, feeling that they would be safer there? Would the man who had broken into the office and emerged empty handed press his quest for them, follow Pierce to his home and try to force him to surrender them? The cattlemen were desperate enough to try anything, he told himself. He darted around the building, wheeled into the alley and ran up its sloping length till he reached the entrance to it, and halted there.

The darkened street, he saw at a glance, was deserted. Slowly, trying to effect a casualness about his movements in case someone was watching, he stepped out onto the planked walk and sauntered upstreet. He glimpsed a man turning into the doorway of a two-story structure some distance up the street from him, and he promptly quickened his pace toward it, broke into a trot when he heard the door close behind the man. As he came up to the building, he saw that there was a vacant store on the street floor, and two doors, one that opened into the store, the other leading to the upper floor. Night light glinted briefly and eerily on the store window. There were dirt smudges on the pane and long furrows through the dirt where rain had struck and streaked it. He tried the second door. It was locked, and he stepped back from it at once, bolted around the building and dashed down the alley that ran alongside. He skidded rather wide around the building at the rear, and narrowly avoided running headlong into a rain barrel that suddenly loomed up in his path. Again there were two doors from which to choose; he chose the one nearest him, found it unlocked, and a moment later he was inside the building.

It was shadowy on the lower floor, and musty smelling. There was a stairway ahead of him; beyond it was the locked street door. He tiptoed forward to the stairway and looked up. A ceiling lamp cast off a small circle of light on the landing, and some of it spilled over the top step and reached about halfway down to the step below it, leaving the rest of the stairway in shadow.

With his hand on his gun, Canavan mounted the stairs and began to climb them. He stopped instantly whenever a step creaked under him; when nothing happened, he climbed higher and finally reached the landing. There was a single door on the upper floor, out of sight from the stairway and from anyone coming up. Thin rays of lamplight seeped out underneath the door and played over the threshold. Canavan crossed the landing on tiptoe. But as he neared the door, he heard a bolt grate, locking it. He frowned; having doors locked in his face was getting annoying. He came up to the door and put his ear to it.

"What . . . what's the meaning of this?" a voice that he recognized at once as Will Pierce's asked. "Who are you and what do you want here? And what's the idea of the neckerchief over your face and that gun that you're pointing at me?"

"I want your record book, Pierce," Canavan heard a man say in a flat, direct voice that didn't sound at all familiar to him.

"My record book?" Pierce echoed.

"That's right. Or whatever it is that you list things in."

"My records happen to be the property of the United States Government," Pierce said, and he sounded indignant about it.

"I still want it," was the curt response. "So trot it out."

"You can't have it."

"This gun says I can, Pierce. And if I have to kill you to get it, then I'll kill you. Now don't tell me that book means more to you than your life? Go on now. Get it so I can get outta here."

"You can't have it," Pierce repeated.

There was sudden movement behind the locked door, sudden sounds of scuffling. A chair was overturned too. But then the scuffling appeared to be over.

"I thought there was something familiar

about you," Canavan heard Pierce say and he sounded a little out of breath. "And now that I've had a look at your face, I know you. I don't know your name, but I know I've seen you around town. You're one of Sturges' crew, aren't you? It doesn't matter though, who you work for, or what your name is. I'm sure a marshal will be able to recognize you from the description I give him and . . ."

There was a sudden, deafening clap of thunder, a roar of gunfire, two, three, four quick shots, a choked-off cry, and the thud of a toppling body striking the floor. There was an oppressive, moment-long silence. Then the bolt was drawn back and the door was yanked open, and Waco burst out. A yellow and green neckerchief covered the lower part of his face. Canavan, whipping out his gun, had backed away from the door and was standing against the far side wall a step away from the stairs. Waco glimpsed him, stared at him as he faltered to an uncertain stop, suddenly flung a shot at him and as Canavan ducked, Waco leaped across the landing. As he flashed by, Canavan thrust out his foot, tripping him. Waco cried out, made a frantic, desperate grab for the banister rail, missed it, and hurtled downward. Canavan wheeled around after him. Waco's plummeting body struck hard about midway down the stairs, landing with a sickening crash on his head and right shoulder. His body arched and flipped over and he rolled down the rest of the way, slipped limply off the bottom step and lay still in the dust that boiled up around him from the lower floor. Holstering his gun, Canavan stepped back from the stairs, spun around and ran into Pierce's quarters.

The throbbing, lifting echoes of gunfire shattered the stillness of the night, and brought Embree and Giffy out of the sheriff's office on the run. They skidded to a stop on the walk and looked up and down the darkened street, trying to locate the direction from which the reports of the shots had come. It was only when two men, one of them white-aproned Tuck Wells, the other Sturges, yelled something from the veranda of the saloon and pointed, that the lawmen began to run. Sturges, cutting across the street, reached the door to Pierce's place a couple of strides ahead of Embree and Giffy. He was trying it, cursing because it refused to open, when the panting sheriff ran up, pushed him aside and put his shoulder to the door. It burst open, and the impetus of Embree's shoulder drive and lunge carried him stumblingly into the hallway to within a step or two of Waco's hunched-over body. Giffy followed him and trampled him, and the sheriff pushed him off roughly.

"You big, clumsy ox," he said thickly.

"How was I supposed to know you were gonna stop so all of a sudden?" Giffy asked crossly. He wheezed and asked: "Who . . . who's that layin' there?"

"Go get a lantern so we can see," Embree ordered.

Giffy trudged out. The sheriff thrust out his arms, barring the way to Sturges and a handful of newcomers who had just run up to the scene and who sought to crowd into the narrow hallway. Turning, and disregarding their grumblings, Embree forced them to back out. Sturges, the most reluctant to give ground, yielded foot by foot and posted himself squarely in front of the open doorway. Presently more men, some of them only half dressed, apparently awakened from their sleep by the shooting, joined the onlookers and milled about with them on the walk, all of them trying at one time or another to get a look inside the hallway only to find that their pushing and neck-craning availed them nothing because the sheriff, standing in front of the limp body, shut it off from their view. Giffy, with a lighted lantern swinging from his hand, and Tuck Wells, with his long apron whipping about and flapping around his ankles, came across the street from the saloon. The bulky deputy, with Wells following at his heels, shouldered his way through the swelling crowd and stepped into the hallway. Embree took the lantern from Giffy, and holding it over Waco, said:

"All right, Giffy. Let's have a look at him. Take that thing off his face."

Giffy grunted, knelt down at Waco's side, lifted the neckerchief and peered under it, took another look, let it drop again hastily, turned his head and looking up at Embree, hissed:

"It's Waco."

Wells, standing a little behind the two lawmen, half turned doorward and called:

"Hey, Sturges! It's your man Waco."

Embree glowered at him over his shoulder.

"How'd you get in here?" he demanded. "Thought I said everybody was to wait outside?"

"That happens to be my lantern you're holding there," Tuck answered evenly.

The sheriff scowled, but he held his tongue. There was renewed shoving outside the door; Sturges had lost his place and had to bull his way through those in front of the door and finally managed to stumble into the hallway. He crowded in between Giffy and Embree and stared down at the body that lay at their feet.

"He's dead," Giffy said without looking up. "Neck's busted. Musta taken a header off the stairs."

The cattleman's mouth opened and his

jaw hung a little. Embree gave him a head-tilted look.

"I don't suppose you'd know, or even have an idea as to what Waco was doing here, would you, Mister Sturges?" he asked, and his voice was heavy with sarcasm. "Huh?"

Sturges' head jerked. His face was beginning to redden.

"Just because he worked for me, that mean he was supposed to come an' tell me every place he was going and what he expected to do there?" he flung back at the sheriff. "I have men workin' for me, full-grown men too, not kids. When their day's work is done and they head for town, what they do with themselves between then and gettin'-up time the next morning is their business."

The sheriff was a little taken aback by Sturges' angry outburst.

"No call for you to get sore about it," he said in a milder tone. "I was only asking, you know."

"I didn't like the way you asked," Sturges retorted.

Giffy climbed to his feet.

"Here," Embree said, and passed the lantern back to him.

He stepped around Waco's body and trudged heavily up the stairs. Near the top, he stopped, bent down and picked up something, took a minute to examine it, then holding it against him so that neither Giffy nor Sturges could see what it was, went on. He stopped again on the landing and seemed to be looking at something on the wall, then he disappeared from view. They heard him moving about on the upper floor; after a couple of minutes they heard a door close overhead, heard his step again, and he reappeared and came down the stairs. He was holding a gun in his hand.

"Thanks for lettin' us use your lantern, Tuck," he said to the bartender. "Soon's we're finished with it, Giffy'll return it to you. So you won't have to wait. You can go on back to your place. Chances are you'll find some customers waiting for you."

Wells looked disappointed. However, he made no comment, simply stalked doorward. When Embree motioned, Giffy followed him, close the door after him, and backed against it. The sheriff held up the gun so that Sturges could see it. He pointed with a thick, stubby finger to four pin-scratched letters in the heel plate.

"W-A-C-O. Spells Waco, right? Then there's no argument about who this gun belonged to."

There was no response from Sturges. His lips appeared to be strangely dry; he moistened them with a quick, nervous, darting movement of his tongue.

"I found Will Pierce layin' upstairs," Embree continued. "Shot dead. Got four slugs in him. Then I found a fifth slug in the wall on the landing, just past the stairs. Now if you want to look for yourself instead of taking my word for it, you'll find there's just one bullet left in it, I don't think there can be any question about where those five shots came from." He tapped the gun butt significantly. "Now what I'd kinda like to know from you is, what was Waco after, did you send him after it, or did he get the idea to get it all by himself and go off on it without telling you anything about it?"

Sturges' tongue darted out again.

"Well?" the sheriff pressed him. "What about it?"

Sturges hesitated. He seemed to be debating something with himself before he answered.

"He was after Pierce's record book," he said.

"That's what I figured," Embree said dryly. "Only I wanted to hear it from you."

"But the idea to go after it was his," Sturges added. "All his, too."

"But since you knew what he was going after," the sheriff pointed out, "and since you stood to profit by it if he got the book away from Pierce, that makes you an . . . an accessory to the crime. Makes you as guilty of what he did as he was. You knew that Pierce was a stubborn old coot, that he wouldn't give up anything, his book or anything else for that matter, just because Waco was holding a gun on him. Chances are the old buzzard dared Waco to shoot. That's the kind he was. But you didn't care. Leastways that's the way it looks, the way the law's gonna look at it. You didn't tell

Waco to forget the idea, did you? You didn't tell him to try to bluff Pierce into handing over the book, and if that didn't work, to let it go rather than make yourself a party to murder, did you? You didn't say anything. You let him go ahead. If Waco had to kill Pierce, that would be too bad for Pierce. Y'know, Sturges, I always thought you were a pretty smart feller. You aren't at all. Fact is, you're downright dumb, and this proves it. D'you know what's gonna happen now?"

"A gover'ment man has been killed," Giffy said from where he was standing, "and it's up to us to get word of it right away to the nearest marshal."

"Right," the sheriff said. "And we haven't any alternative about it, either. We've got to do it. And when a marshal hits town and starts pokin' his nose into things, you're gonna be in trouble. Bad trouble, too."

"Yeah?" Sturges flung at him defiantly.

"Yeah. Because we won't do anything to cover up for you."

"I think you will, Embree," Sturges said

quietly. "Fact is, I know you will. And you wanna know why? Because your hands aren't any cleaner than mine are. Because I've got witnesses who'll swear same as I will, if you force our hand, that you offered to cover up for us when we make our sweep against the nesters. So, if you don't want to get yourself in trouble, you'd better fix up a story you can tell that marshal when he hits Cuero that'll satisfy him and send him on his way again. For instance, you might tell him that Waco got the cockeyed idea that Pierce had a lot o' gover'ment dough on him or hid away up at his place and that Waco must've decided to steal it. The fact that Pierce didn't have it, and that Waco must've lost his head and killed him, well, that's tough because Pierce was a good man. But being that Waco got himself killed running out've Pierce's place, that sorta makes it an eye for an eye, and oughta satisfy the law. 'Course that's only a suggestion, you understand. You think it over, and use it if you like, or maybe cook up something you think might sound even better. That's up to you. But as far as I'm concerned, I'm in the clear because I didn't know a blamed thing about what Waco was up to. And you're gonna back me up on that."

He walked doorward. Giffy stepped aside to let him pass, closed the door after he had gone and backed against it again, and lifted his eyes to meet Embree's.

9

BECAUSE he was curious about the outcome of Will Pierce's murder, and because he wondered what sort of explanation would be given out to cover it, Canavan rode townward early the next day. He loped into Cuero, slowed Aggie to a trot as they came down the street, and headed for the saloon. If anyone could tell him what he wanted to know, it would be Tuck Wells. Bartenders, it was generally agreed, were usually the best informed individuals in any town, and Wells, he had already found, was no exception. Nearing the saloon, Canavan spied Tuck. He was sweeping the veranda. Canavan pulled up at the curb, slacked a little in the saddle, and called:

"Hi."

"Hi, partner," Wells acknowledged, and mechanically lifted his right arm in his customary half-salute.

Canavan swung down, flipped Aggie's reins loosely around the rail, mounted the walk and sauntered across it, and leisurely climbed the steps.

"You missed some excitement 'round here last night," Wells told him, leaning on his broom.

"That so?"

"Yep," the bartender went on. "Will Pierce, the old feller who ran the gover'-ment Land Office, was killed."

"You don't say!"

When Wells turned and trudged inside, Canavan followed him. Tuck put away his broom and took his place behind the bar. Canavan hunched over it.

"What happened?" he asked.

"Oh, seems some damned fool, a feller named Waco, leastways that's what he called himself, got it into his head that Pierce had a whole bundle of gover'ment dough stashed away up at his place. Where he lived, I mean. Not the office. Anyway, this Waco tried to scare Pierce into handing it over, and when Pierce wouldn't do it, Waco just about blasted him apart."

222

"I'll be doggoned!"

"But things have a funny way of evening themselves up. Y'know?"

"How do you mean?"

"Well, here's a for-instance. Busting out've Pierce's place after killing him, Waco took a header off the stairs, he was going so fast, and broke his fool neck."

"Guess he got what was coming to him then. Did he get the dough he was after?"

"Nope," Wells replied with a grim shake of his head. "Not one red cent. Whoever gave him the idea that Pierce had any dough hid away sure gave him a wrong steer. The sheriff went through both places, Pierce's place as well as the office, just to be sure, y'know, but he couldn't find anything worth talking about. Just a couple o' bucks in Pierce's pants pockets. Then he went over to the bank and they told him that every time Pierce took in any dough, he always hustled it over and deposited it. Guess he wasn't taking any chances on anything happening to the gover'ment's money."

Canavan made no interrupting comment, but Wells paused anyway in his recital.

"Too bad about Pierce though," he said shortly, with another shake of his head. "I never got to know him too well, being that he never came in here. I knew him to say hello to and sometimes pass the time o' day with, but that was all. But some of the folks around got friendly with him, and they liked him, say he was kinda straight-laced, but pretty regular otherwise."

"Uh-huh."

"The gover'ment's gonna have a tough time of it, all right, getting somebody to take his place. The job doesn't pay much, and if the feller who takes it is married and has a family to look out for, he's gonna find it tough getting along on his pay. Pierce made out because he didn't have anybody 'cept himself to worry about. Anyway, that's what happened around here last night. How are things with you?"

"O-h, so-so."

"Been managing to hold your own though, haven't you?"

Canavan grinned.

"So far I have."

"Then I'd say you're doing all right," Wells assured him. Emerging from behind the bar when Canavan straightened up, he followed Canavan out to the veranda, glanced skyward for a moment, and remarked: "Looks like it's gonna be a nice day."

"Yeah," Canavan said, hitching up his levis. "Looks like it, all right."

He went down the steps to the walk and out to the curb, untied Aggie and climbed up into the saddle and wheeled the mare, responded to Wells' salute with a wave of his hand, and rode up the street. Minutes later Cuero was behind him and rapidly fading out of sight. About a mile from town, Canavan heard hoofbeats behind him and he twisted around and looked back. He spotted an oncoming horseman, but the distance between them was too great to permit recognition. Aggie wanted to run, but Canavan held her down, made her lope instead of gallop. He looked back a couple of times, and finally recognized the

225

approaching horseman. It was the sheriff. Slowing Aggie despite her objections, Canavan permitted Embree to overtake him. The lawman came drumming up alongside of him and, recognizing him, promptly slowed his mount to match Aggie's trot. Neither man voiced a greeting or even signalled one.

"I was going out to the Fisher place," Embree began. "To see you."

"Me?" Canavan repeated in surprise. He gave Embree a searching look. "What about?"

He pulled back on the reins and brought Aggie to a full stop. The sheriff pulled up too. Canavan turned to him.

"What'd you want to see me about?"

Embree delayed answering for a moment, then he said:

"We don't have to talk out here, do we? In the middle of the road?"

Canavan shrugged, and nudging Aggie with his knees, walked her off to the side of the road; the sheriff followed and reined in alongside of him again, and said:

"Thought you might want to know that

226

the cattlemen are getting together to make a sweep against the nesters."

Canavan looked hard at him.

"So Nye's finally set to make his big play, huh?"

"Nye isn't in on this," Embree answered rather stiffly.

Canavan grinned a little.

"Won't he feel slighted when he hears about it? How come he wasn't invited to take a hand?"

"He was," the sheriff said evenly. "Only he turned it down."

"Well, good for him!"

"He turned it down," Embree continued, "because the nesters don't mean anything to him. When he's set to go, it won't be after them. It'll be after you."

"I see," Canavan said. "Then who . . . ?"

"It's Sturges who's leading the sweep. He and Fleming are rounding up a bunch of men, and when they're ready, the word will go out and they'll all start riding."

"Got any idea when that might be?"

"The way I got it, it's supposed to be set for some time tomorrow night."

"Uh-huh," Canavan said thoughtfully. "Probably figure to hit us when they expect we'll be asleep. Thanks for letting us know, Embree."

They sat in silence then, for a long, rather awkward moment; when the silence and Canavan's steady gaze began to make the sheriff feel uncomfortable, he flushed a bit.

"What are you lookin' at me like that for?"

"I don't get it, Embree. I don't understand it, why you should go outta your way to do something like this for the nesters."

"Can't a man do what he thinks he oughta without making a fuss about it, or without somebody else making the to-do?"

"I didn't think you had any more use for the nesters than the cattlemen. So how come this all-of-a-sudden change in you?"

Embree's face suddenly flamed, and he sputtered:

"If you don't want to take this the way I'm giving it to you . . ."

"You have a falling out or something

with the cattlemen, and is this your way of getting back at them?"

"I didn't have any falling out with anybody," the sheriff said flatly, still red-faced.

"All right," Canavan said with a lift of his hands and shoulders. "You oughta know. If you say you didn't, that's good enough for me."

The crimson began to fade out of Embree's face, leaving it only slightly red-tinged.

"Like I said," he went on again, "Sturges is the one leading the sweep even though Fleming's the one who's been out doing the talking to the cattlemen and the rounding up of the men. Without Sturges and Fleming to stir them up, the others would probably hate the guts and the sight of the nesters, but that's about as far as it would go. 'Course that trick you pulled on them, getting the nesters to file on their grazing lands, that hasn't helped matters any. That's what's made them willing to listen to Fleming and go in on this. Anyway, that's it, Canavan. If you come out've this thing tomorrow night, you'll still have Nye to deal with."

Canavan smiled thinly.

"Mind if I worry about one thing at a time?" he asked.

The sheriff disregarded it and continued:

"He's got a lot to square up with you, and knowing Nye the way I do, I know he won't rest till he pays you back good. But that's the way you been asking for it."

"That's right. So whatever happens to me will be my tough luck."

"Gotta get back to town," Embree said.

"Thanks again."

"Yeah, sure," the sheriff said, wheeled away from Canavan, stopped again and said: "If your nesters hope to have any peace around here, you'd better let them know that Sturges is the man who's standing in the way of it. So it will have to be him or them, and it can't be both because he won't let it be that way. That shouldn't be too hard for them to understand, and it oughta help them make up their minds to what they've got to do. Unless, of course," and his eyes suddenly seemed to smile, "you take it on yourself and do it for them. It wouldn't mean much to you, just another notch on your gun butt. But think what it would mean to them, to the nesters, and to their families. They could stop running, and they could settle down. But that's for you to decide, Canavan. Well, so long."

"So long, Embree."

Canavan watched the sheriff ride away, followed him with narrowed eyes till he was out of sight, then he sat back in the saddle. Aggie turned her head and looked around at him wonderingly, but he paid no attention to her. She pawed the ground, still he sat motionlessly.

"The son-uva-gun!" he thought to himself. "The gall of him! Finally worked up enough courage to come out with it. I knew all along he didn't come out here to warn us about the sweep because he was concerned about the nesters and didn't want to see anything happen to them. That was just a cover-up for what he really wants, to have Sturges killed off. And I know damned well he doesn't want that just because of what Sturges has been up to, stirring up feeling against the nesters. It's for some other reason, something more important to him, something personal between him and Sturges. And if he can get us to get rid of Sturges for him, he'll be the smart one. Well, we'll have to see about that, whether it'll be to our advantage to get Sturges, or grab him off and use him to show up Embree for what he really is. But what's got me wondering is what coulda happened that soured him on Sturges, and if it had anything to do with that Pierce killing?"

He thought about it a while longer. Finally, with a lift of his shoulders, a sign that thinking about it hadn't produced any helpful ideas, he wheeled Aggie, guided her back into the middle of the road. But he refused to let her have her own way about it; despite her eagerness to run, he held her in check, made her canter instead of gallop. She snorted and tossed her head and made a noisy to-do; when he had had enough of it, he jerked the reins and spoke sharply to her, and recognizing the signs that he was in no mood for her antics, she subsided and obeyed him without any further display of temper. It was just about the same time that he was wheeling into the cut-through that led to the Fisher homestead, that the sheriff, returned to Cuero, was dismounting in front of his office.

Giffy had taken over the desk, filling the chair behind it as bulkily as Embree did. He was sitting hunched forward over the desk with his chin resting on his folded arms, when the door opened and Embree came striding in. Giffy raised his eyes. When he saw that it was the sheriff, he jerked back and started to heave himself up only to have Embree motion to him to stay where he was. Giffy slumped down again. The sheriff came up to the desk.

"How'd you make out?" Giffy asked. "Did you see him?"

"'Course I saw him," Embree answered a little tartly. He thumbed his hat up from his forehead, took it off and laid it on the desk. "And I think I made out all right with him, too."

"Y'mean he's gonna go after Sturges himself?"

"Yeah, I kinda think he will, Giff.

'Specially after the way I put it to him."

"Good," Giffy said, nodding. "Be a cinch for him, y'know, to get Sturges, if he really goes out to get him? Sturges is slower'n molasses when it comes to gunplay, and Canavan oughta be able to beat him to the draw a dozen ways from Sunday."

"I'll breathe a lot easier when I know it's done," Embree said.

"I know." But then as an afterthought, Giffy asked: "What about Fleming?"

"Oh, he doesn't count! Neither do the other two, Booth and Kiley, even though they were all here and heard me say I'd cover up for them when they went after the nesters. I can handle them."

Giffy offered no opinion. Instead he asked:

"Anything we can do to help things along, to get them moving faster?"

"No," he said. "Not a thing. It's all up to Canavan, and all we can do is sit tight and wait and hope it all goes off the way I'd like it to."

"Uh-huh."

"Now how about you haulin' yourself up from there and letting me sit down?"

At Canavan's instance, once the homesteader's claims had been accepted and registered, a property line was begun. Normally it would have taken the form of a fence, the usual dividing line between properties. But Canavan knew that a fence wouldn't last very long; Sturges' crew would see to that. So he decided upon something of a more permanent nature, a rock barrier that started at the cut-through, and passing behind Fisher's barn, stretched away northward. Pierce had provided a map of the homesteader's holdings on which he had painstakingly marked off the boundaries between the cattlemen's spreads. Sturges', Fleming's, Booth's, Kiley's and Weber's, and what was now Fisher's property and that which the other homesteaders had laid claim to. The map was followed religiously so as to avoid disputes later on. The rocks that formed the barrier were of varying sizes and shapes. Some of them required the combined efforts of two men to uproot them and roll them into position in the line; some were so big that they had to be roped and then hauled into place by horses. The women members of the party insisted upon participating in the project, and they brought smaller rocks and laid them on top of the big ones and helped raise the height of the barrier. It was a back-breaking task, and one that was just as toll-exacting on fingers and fingernails. But it was done with such surprising willingness that Canavan couldn't help but admire them for their spirit. His eyes lingered the longest on Molly, who toiled manfully with the others. Once when she came trudging by, red-faced from her exertions and her cheek dirt-smudged, she stopped, looked at him and smiled and remarked:

"Even young Johnny's doing his share. He hunts up the rocks and leads us to them."

"He's all right," Canavan told her gravely.

"I told you, didn't I, that what we needed most was someone to lead us, to tell us what to do, and that we'd do it willingly?"

"I've no complaints, Molly."

"I'm glad," she said simply, and trudged off after Johnny.

Only Doreen Gregg declined to join the others in the man-sized undertaking. She was standing near her wagon, watching the barrier continue to grow, when Canavan, striding by, stopped and looked around at her and retraced his steps to her side.

"In case you're wondering why I've refused to help with the building of that wall," she said, "I'm planning to leave here."

"That so? Heading for California like you said, huh?"

"I'm going to find a place for myself in town."

"I see."

"I'll probably be staying at the hotel for a time," she went on. "When you're in town . . ."

"Thanks. But when I go to town, I don't usually have time for visiting."

"If I were someone else, you'd find time though, wouldn't you?" she chided him, smiling as she always did when she wanted to take the edge off her words, yet still achieve their cutting effect.

"If you were someone else like who?" he pressed her.

She didn't answer. She flushed a little under his steady gaze, even averted her eyes for the moment.

"Yeah, come to think of it, I suppose if you were someone else, I'd manage to find the time to stop and see you," he went on deliberately. When it failed to draw the response he sought, he added in the same tone: "I don't like people who hint at things because they haven't got the guts to come right out with them."

She raised her eyes.

"All right," she said. "If you insist. If I were Molly Fisher, you'd find time for me, wouldn't you?"

"So that's it!"

"Yes," she said calmly. "I know whose friend you are, and I know it isn't Reuben's because he doesn't like you. In fact, he dislikes you. And I think I know why. Because he suspects there's something between you and his wife."

His lips came together and thinned.

"And there is, isn't there?" She suddenly laughed, a laugh that was a little too gay and too taunting, and his eyes glinted. "Oh, that look in your eyes! If I were a man, you'd kill me for that, wouldn't you? Isn't that what you're known for, that you're a killer?"

He walked away from her. She ran after him.

"Canavan . . . please!"

He stopped and looked back at her. She came running up to him, lifted her face to him.

"I'm sorry," she breathed at him. "Honestly and terribly sorry. I shouldn't have said what I did. Any of it. I hadn't any right to."

"It's all right."

"Then you forgive me?" she asked eagerly, her hands on his forearms. "Then we'll still be friends?"

"Another kind o' people I haven't any use for are those who say things out've pure meanness, and when they've had their say and the damage is done, make a big show of being sorry. You're one of those people, Doreen."

She stepped back from him.

"Indeed!" she said. "Then I'm not sorry at all. In fact, I'm glad, awfully glad, too."

"That's what I figured."

Her eyes were burning.

"I don't like you, Canavan," she said angrily.

"That's all right," he replied. "I don't like you either. So we're even."

She glowered and he laughed at her, and suddenly, enraged. . . .

"You . . . you swine!"

She raised her hand and slapped him. He had seen the slap coming and he could have avoided it quite easily, but he didn't, took it without moving, without the barest twitch of a muscle. But then his own hand flashed upward and he slapped her stingingly, left the red imprint of his hand on her cheek. Open-mouthed she stared at him, lifted her hand mechanically to her cheek.

"Well?" he taunted. "Want to go 'round

again? You can go first again if you want to."

She gasped, spun around and ran back to her wagon. Her horses were tied to the rear wheel. She untied them and led them forward, backed them into the traces and hitched them up, then raising her skirts she climbed up to the high seat. She unwound the reins from around the handbrake, released it, flicked the loose ends of the reins over the horses' heads, startling them into movement. They strained against the traces and the wagon lurched a little; she lashed the horses and they strained again.

This time the big wheels turned, bit into the hard-packed ground, and the wagon moved, pulled out of line. Doreen's crimsoned face was a reflection of fury. She glared at Canavan and drove straight at him. As the lumbering wagon neared him, he stepped back. When it came abreast of him, Doreen leaned down from the driver's seat and lashed at him with the reins, screamed at him when he avoided them. Men and women alike, even young Johnny Fisher, stopped instantly whatever it was that they were doing and looked in the direction of the trundling wagon as it rolled by, heading for the open road beyond the cut-through. Then their eyes, wide and wondering, shifted to Canavan and held on him. Reuben Fisher, mopping his sweaty, grimy face with a bandana, trudged up to him.

"What happened?" he asked. "What was that all about, and where's Doreen going?"

Canavan, turning, met his eyes.

"She's above lending a hand like the other women are doing," he replied. "So she's taken herself off to town."

Fisher looked surprised.

"But she'll be back, won't she?"

"No, I don't think she will."

"But what is she going to do in town?"

"Stay there. At least, for the time being. Till she decides to go elsewhere. There's nothing out here for her. You folks can't give her what she wants, what she's looking for."

"But we're her friends," the homesteader protested. "To go off like that, without a goodbye or even a word of explanation . . ."

"Maybe it was better that way. Easier all around, for her, for you people."

Fisher looked at him blankly. But he did not ask the question that Canavan expected of him. Instead he blurted out:

"Well, whatever it is that she wants, does she think she'll find it among strangers?"

"I think she stands a far better chance there than she does here," Canavan answered and walked off.

He could feel Fisher's eyes on him, holding on him, following him, and he knew that the homesteader did not understand. But he had had enough of Doreen Gregg, and he had no desire to discuss her, last of all with Reuben Fisher. As he sauntered toward the barrier he noticed in one sweeping glance that the men had resumed their work, and that the line of rocks had passed the house. But the women, standing about singly and in pairs at various points along the barrier, were looking at him in the same curious and wondering way in which Fisher had eyed him. He swerved away toward the house and came up to the barrier and followed it, thinking to himself:

"Doreen isn't like these nester women. They don't ask much out've life, 'cept just a chance to live fairly decently, and they're willing to work hard, struggle if necessary, even suffer for that chance. That isn't for Doreen. She wants much more out've life, a lot more, and how she gets it doesn't matter."

He had recognized her for what she was the first time he had seen her because he had seen her kind many times before, in New Orleans, in the border towns in both Texas and Mexico, and in the gold towns in California. Wherever there was excitement, sometimes only the promise of it, these women were bound to appear because they lived for excitement and searched for it constantly. They moved about from place to place, and from man to man. They paid the price that was asked of them, but they never quite got what they were looking for. Then the years as well as the lives they led exacted a toll of them; all too soon and much too suddenly, they found that they had lost their attractiveness. They were cast off, replaced by younger, fresher women. There was no turning back then; it was too late to return to the way of life which they had rejected and abandoned. For a time they hovered about on the fringe of things, then, pushed farther back all the time into the background, they withdrew themselves completely. Disappointed and disillusioned and in many instances broken in health as well as in spirit, and generally penniless, they disappeared, and were never seen or heard from again. That was the way Doreen Gregg would wind up, Canavan told himself grimly.

It was evening. The lengthening shadows had already begun to deepen over Cuero. Standing in the open doorway of the sheriff's office, Giffy watched night come on, saw the stores darken and lose their identity in the veiling darkness, saw the street begin to empty as the townspeople made their way homeward. Giffy watched it with the detached interest of an onlooker who had seen the same thing happen with such monotonous regularity and sameness that the transition from evening to night meant little to him but that bedtime was getting closer. He had had his supper and now he was waiting for Embree to return from his. They would sit around in the turned-down lamplight in the office, talk idly about this and that, and after a while conversation would die out. The sheriff would be the first to nod and doze; once Giffy heard Embree's heavy breathing, he would doze off too. Then around nine he would wake and get up, go to the door and bolt it, and the sheriff would hear the creak of the warped floorboards under him and he would wake too.

The conversation that followed this piece of business was always about the same. This is the way it usually ran.

"Guess I musta dozed off," Embree would say in a rather sheepish and apologetic tone.

It was said that way deliberately. It was a cue to Giffy who, knowing what was expected of him, always snatched it up alertly, and who promptly said:

"So what? Don't I always tell you the same thing every night, that a man's got the right to feel plumb wore out after he puts in a full day the way you do?"

Giffy said it as though he had memorized it, and since he had to say it every night the words spilled out of him almost mechanically. Wisely he spoke his piece with a straight face, so the sheriff never had any reason to doubt his sincerity. His defense of Embree made the latter feel better, even to the point of bestowing a kindly smile upon his appreciative deputy. The fact that Giffy put in the same number of hours that the sheriff devoted to their work, and Embree's curious failure to take note of it and make mention of it, even offhandedly, should have made Giffy unhappy. That it didn't was due to the full measure of satisfaction that he derived in other ways. The first was that Embree did not even suspect that Giffy napped nightly too. The second was this: despite the fact that the two men looked to be about the same age and probably were, Giffy always stoutly maintained that he was the younger. By letting the sheriff think that he, Giffy, was the better able of the two to withstand the rigors of their work, Giffy felt that he was proving his contention. A younger man, he was not unwilling to point out, did not tire as quickly as an older man did, and Embree's apparent willingness to accept his claim filled Giffy's cup to its fullest.

Embree would yawn and stretch mightily, rub his nose and scratch his head, and finally, with a wearied sigh, say:

"How about we call it a day, Giff?"

It was "Giff" when Embree felt kindly disposed toward his deputy, and "Giffy" when he was put out with him.

"Might as well, I suppose."

"After nine, isn't it?"

"Yeah, sure. More'n a quarter after now."

Embree would struggle up into a sitting position.

"Quarter after, huh? Then what are we waiting for?"

"For you to get up from there," Giffy would answer with a grin.

"Be a good feller and lock up."

"Door's locked already. Soon's you get a move on, I'll douse the light in here."

Embree would grunt and hoist himself up from his chair, and the squeak that came from it was probably the chair's way of expressing its relief. When he plodded into the back room, their living quarters, the light in the office proper would go out, and Giffy would troop after the sheriff and close the connecting door behind him.

Giffy's attention was attracted by the sound of drumming hoofs. He poked his head out, ranged his gaze upstreet in the direction of the hoofbeats. A horseman, shadowy and unrecognizable in the night light, came into view. Giffy's eyes focused on him, held on him as he came loping down the street. He watched the man ride up to the saloon, pull up at the curb and dismount, saw him stand idly on the walk for a moment or two, then cross it and climb the steps to the veranda. Topping the steps, he halted again, within the lights that came from the saloon and which played over the veranda. Giffy recognized him at once. It was Canavan.

"Bet he's come to get Sturges," Giffy murmured to himself, and instantly excitement began to build within him. "Gee, I wish Embree would get back. Then I could go see it happen."

As he watched, Canavan trudged into the saloon.

But there was no sign yet of the sheriff, and Giffy began to get impatient and fidgety. He kept his gaze fixed on the saloon, unwilling to take his eyes from it for even the barest instant, as though he were afraid that if he glanced away something might happen there before he could get upstreet to witness it. Nervousness brought on by his steadily mounting excitement made him bite his lip. But after a couple of tensed minutes passed uneventfully, he began to wonder. He couldn't understand it. Why hadn't something happened? Sturges was a nightly visitor to Cuero, so it couldn't be due to him that he wasn't there. The silence and the delay had to be due to something else. Giffy thought about it; suddenly his frowning expression relaxed, an indication that he had come up with an explanation. Canavan, he told himself, was simply waiting for the right moment to make his move. The saloon was probably crowded, and Giffy, picturing it to himself, envisioned the bar thronged with noisy, clamorous men standing two and perhaps three deep in front of it, with Sturges among them, unaware of Canavan's presence and his reason for being there, surrounded by other cattlemen and shut off by them from Canavan's view. He could see Canavan too, standing off to a side, staying his hand till some of the customers had departed. A few of them were doubtless townsmen; but the majority were cattlemen, and they would naturally spring to Sturges' defense if Canavan sought to jump him while they were there. So it was reasonable to assume that Canavan was merely biding his time, waiting for the crowd to thin out.

But then suddenly, and with a let-down feeling, Giffy noticed that there weren't any horses tied up in front of the saloon, and ranging his gaze about a little wildly, saw that there weren't any horses tied up at any of the other rails along the street. Forced to concede then that his theory was wrong, Giffy abandoned it and sought another. Could it be, he asked himself, that for the first time in a long, long time, probably a span of years, Sturges had failed to make his nightly visit to Cuero? It didn't seem possible, hence Giffy rejected the idea. He was more inclined to believe that Sturges had simply been delayed, and would show up in Cuero eventually. Reassured again, Giffy was able to bridle and control his impatience. It was just as well that Sturges was late; it would give Embree even more time to have his supper and return to the office. But then another disturbing thought came to Giffy. It revolved around Canavan. Giffy hoped Canavan wouldn't tire of waiting for Sturges to appear and decide to put off his mission for another time.

Suddenly there was a startling, silence-shattering, carrying echo of gunfire from somewhere off in the dark distance beyond the town. Instantly Giffy was out of the

252

doorway and standing tensely in the very middle of the walk and staring upstreet with wide eyes. He shot a worried look at the saloon, saw a tall figure that he knew at once was Canavan come rushing out, saw him scurry down the steps to the walk and out to the curb, saw him leap up on his horse's back, wheel and dash off. Disappointed at this turn of events, Giffy did not notice the man who came hurrying across the street till he stepped up on the walk, and halting at Giffy's side, wheezed:

"They tricked me." Giffy's head jerked around and he stared blankly at Embree. "They lied to me, the dirty bastids. They told me it was gonna be tomorrow night."

By then Giffy was himself again.

"Well, you'd better prepare yourself for what's bound to follow this," he told the sheriff grimly. "'Less I miss my guess, there's gonna be hell to pay around here. If you think Canavan ran wild when they killed his wife, wait and see what happens when he gets going this time. He's got it in for the cattlemen, and he'll pay them back good. You see if he don't."

"You wanna know something, Giffy?" the sheriff shot back at him. "He can run as wild as he likes, and we won't do a damned thing to stop him, or even slow him down. And if the range runs red with blood, the cattlemen'll have nobody 'cept themselves to blame it on."

He turned away and strode into the office. Giffy wheeled around after him and followed him inside. The door slammed and a bolt rasped as it was shoved through the brackets. Standing in the connecting doorway, Embree looked at Giffy over his shoulder and said:

"I still don't know what to do about notifying a marshal. Whether we oughta do it or hold off a while."

"We're supposed to do it right off, aren't we?"

"That's what we're supposed to do. But supposing something comes up and we don't get around to it as soon as we'd like to?"

"Then we hold off till we're free to do it."

The sheriff grunted.

"Then I think that's what we'll do. Hold off a while."

The light in the office went out. The building that housed the office melted back, faded away into the surrounding and deepening darkness. Men appeared in the street, a handful of them. They came together and stood about talking among themselves. When one of them happened to turn and looked downstreet, and noted that the sheriff's office was dark, he called attention to it. Apparently satisfied that the shooting that they had heard had no particular significance, judging by the fact that the sheriff didn't think enough of it to warrant his doing anything about it, the men parted and trudged back to their homes. A door closed here, another slammed somewhere else along the street, then everything was hushed again.

10

THE Sturges-Fleming sweep against the intruding and unwanted homesteaders was over, and to all intents and purposes the cattlemen had won an unchallenged victory. The homesteaders, taken completely by surprise, had offered no resistance, not even token resistance. Now they stood bunched together in a tight little group, with mounted men, brandishing their guns, forming a circle around them. There was concern in the men's faces, and fright in the women's and children's, and a tight-mouthed grimness in the faces of their captors. Four of the raiders lay dead despite the fact that not a single homesteader shot had been fired at the invaders.

Thundering across the darkened range at the Fisher place because it was known that the homesteaders had taken refuge there, their hard-riding surge had carried them headlong into the rock barrier that suddenly loomed up in front of them. It was too late for the massed horsemen to pull up or swerve away from it; those directly behind the lead rank piled into it, drove it into the rocks. Men were thrown, catapulted over their horses' heads as the panic-stricken animals crashed into the barrier and fell brokenly. Too stunned by the force with which they were hurled from their saddles, and unable to twist away from the threshing legs and the lashing hoofs of the injured horses, four men's lives were snuffed out. One man was kicked to death, another trampled, and two others crushed when their felled horses rolled over on them.

Wild, aimless and uncalled-for shooting flared for a moment when a couple of horsemen panicked and fired at imaginary targets, adding to the confusion. More fatalities might have resulted if the last band of horsemen had followed the lead of those ahead of it; but it had held back a little, hence it was able to pull up sharply and swerve away. Swinging northward and following the barrier, it wheeled around the last rock that the homesteaders had rolled into position in the line, and came thundering down upon the drawn-up wagons at a full gallop just as the homesteaders were climbing down from them. It was a fairly simple matter for the dozen or so horsemen to cow their victims into submission and herd them together.

The cries of the injured lifted above all other sounds and noises. Wagon lanterns were hurriedly commandeered and lighted; minutes later, yellowish, eerie light was flooding the area on the far side of the barrier where searchers were picking their way gingerly through the tangle of men's and horses' bodies. The dead were left untouched. The injured horses were promptly disposed of, dispatched by gunfire, to save them from any further suffering and to make certain that they did no more harm by their agonized threshing about to the men who lay near them. The latter were lifted and carried away and laid in the lush grass beyond the spot. Those who could manage it by themselves limped about, sought out men from their own crews, climbed up behind them, and were ridden away so that their injuries could be treated. Those who had suffered more serious hurts were hoisted up in front of horsemen who promptly wheeled away with them and took them to town for professional medical help.

Fleming, who had supervised the removal of the injured men, rode around the barrier and pulled up in front of the house where he spied Sturges standing near the open door, twisting a handful of twigs into a faggot. Fleming climbed down, stepped around Sturges, and peered into the house.

"They're down there," Sturges told him, half turning and nodding in the direction of the wagons. "With the others. How bad did we get it pilin' into that wall?"

"Bad," Fleming replied. "We lost four men and six horses. Couple o' men got themselves pretty well banged up."

Sturges touched a lighted match to the faggot, and when it began to burn he pushed Fleming out of the way and tossed the sputtering firebrand into the house. A second faggot was thrown inside, then a third. The flimsy structure caught fire.

Through the open door they could see flames whipping about, leaping across the floor, swarming over the place in waves. Suddenly there was a strange, crackling sound, and Sturges and Fleming looked at each other questioningly; when neither man could offer an explanation, both raised their eyes in search of one. They saw tongues of flame burst through the roof, saw showers of sparks leap upward from it and bomb the night sky, and they hastily retreated. Fleming glimpsed his horse trotting away toward the barn. Soon flames broke through the walls, and the two men backed off still further. Glancing skyward, Fleming saw a glow deepening overhead, a reflection of the fire. Sturges was staring at the burning house, apparently fascinated by the curling flames.

"What d'we do now?" Fleming asked him.

"Huh?"

"What are we gonna do with these nesters?"

Sturges' head jerked around.

"What d'you think we're gonna do with

260

them?" he demanded. "Think we came after them just to chase them away?"

Fleming gave him a quick, searching look.

"You mean we're gonna kill them?" he asked.

Sturges didn't answer.

"The women and children too?"

"If we let a single nester, man, woman or kid get away," Sturges said bluntly, "we'll be loopin' a rope around our necks. Just let one of th'm stay alive and get to a marshal and spill what happened to the rest of them, and we'll swing for it. But if we go through with it the way we planned it, we'll be all right. Kill them all off, then there won't be any witnesses to testify against us."

Fleming looked troubled.

"Thought we were only going after the men?"

"I dunno where you got that idea," Sturges replied. "I know damned well you didn't get it from me. When we got together, it was to get rid of the nesters, and there wasn't anything said about it being just the men. Far as I'm concerned, a nester

261

is a nester, and it doesn't make a damned bit o' difference whether it's a man or a woman or even a kid. They're all alike to me. And when we talked about it, you were so het up about getting rid of the nesters, I took it for granted you felt the same way about them that I did. But now alluva sudden, now that we've got them where we want them, you're singin' a different tune. I dunno what you thought we were gonna do once we got all those men together and we started riding over here. Maybe you thought we were just gonna throw a scare . . . ?"

"All I'm saying is that I don't like the idea of butchering a lot o' women and kids."

"Then you'd better get to like it," Sturges retorted.

"We aren't Indians out to massacre a wagon train," Fleming said doggedly.

Sturges squared around to him.

"Wanna tell you something, Fleming," he began curtly. "Whether you like the idea or you don't, every nester in that bunch will be dead before this night is over. Now that you know what we're gonna do, if you haven't got the guts or the belly to go through with what you helped start, you can pull out. But get this, Fleming. Whether you stay or you pull out, you're in this same as I am, right smack up to our necks. If anything ever comes up and I get grabbed by a marshal, you can bet everything you got or ever will have that whatever they do to me, they'll do to you too. Because I'll tell the law you had just as much to do with this as I did. Now you make up your mind, if you've got one, to what you wanna do. Meanwhile I've got things to do and I'm gonna get at them."

He started away. Fleming overtook him, and trudging along with him, said unhappily:

"If they'da put up a fight and we killed them all, that woulda been different."

"I know, and that woulda made things easier for us. But they didn't put up a fight. So we haven't any . . . any alternative. We have to go through with getting rid of them the only way that's open to us."

This time there was no protest by Fleming. Apparently he had resigned himself

263

to accepting the situation. After a brief silence, he asked:

"No sign of that troublemaker, huh?"

"Who d'you mean, Canavan?"

"'Course. He was the one who started this business, getting the nesters to act up, wasn't he?"

"No sign of him."

"Then even if we kill off every one of the nesters," Fleming said and there was sudden hopefulness in his voice, "we still won't be any better off than we were before tonight. Right? We'll still have Canavan to deal with."

"Maybe, maybe not," Sturges said. "I know Coley Nye, and I know that when he sets out to do something, he usually does it. So I think we can count on him takin' care of Canavan for us."

"But supposing he doesn't?" Fleming pressed him. "Suppose it works out the other way 'round, that Canavan gets Nye? What happens to us then? What d'we do then?"

"Oh, for Pete's sake, Fleming!"

"I know, but I'd still like to know what

you've got in mind for then, just in case."

"Can't tell you that because I haven't even thought that far ahead."

"H'm," Fleming said darkly. "That's what I figured. Trouble with you, Sturges, is that you think only of now instead of planning for tomorrow too and for the day after that."

"Suppose," Sturges said, ignoring Fleming's criticism, "that instead of lookin' so far ahead and borrowing trouble when we don't know that there's gonna be any, that we do what we have to do now, and then wait and see what happens afterward? If anything comes up then, we'll just have to face up to it and meet it the best way we can. So quit worrying when you don't have to."

"Still think Embree will cover up for us for tonight?"

"I know damned well he will!"

"I wish I could be as sure of that as you are."

"I'm telling you he will," Sturges insisted, "because he knows what's good for him."

Despite the latter's assurances, Fleming's expression showed that he wasn't as fully satisfied with things as Sturges seemed to think he should be. But the fact that he did not pursue the discussion indicated a realization on his part that he had no alternative but to go along with Sturges, and hope for the best.

As they neared the wagons, he asked:

"Where are you gonna do it? Hope you don't aim to do it here?"

"No, 'course not," Sturges answered. "This is too close to town. We'll take them out on the range a couple o' miles and find a place there. 'Course a river would be better if there was one around, a good, deep one. Or a ravine."

"A ravine?" Fleming repeated. "What's the matter with the one on what used to be old man Sleiger's place? Nobody lives there now. Fact is, nobody's lived on the place since Sleiger died."

"Hey, that's right, Fleming! That'd be just the place for it."

Fleming looked hard at Sturges, and knew at once what he was thinking.

In the not too distant past, when bands of

lawless whites who could be more ruthless than the Indians who roamed the prairies, it was not uncommon for them to attack a wagon train if they thought it looked as though it might prove to be a worthwhile haul. They would massacre everyone in the train, rob the dead of their possessions, sometimes even of their clothes if they were worth reselling, then they would tumble the half-denuded bodies into a ravine. The wagons were set afire and the horses taken or driven off. No one cared very much, and no one even wondered, much less undertook to search for the hapless members of the train. It was only when another train came upon the burned-out hulks of the wagons that the unfortunate incident came to light. The second train simply redoubled its vigilance as it got under way again.

"We'll do the right thing by them though," Sturges said and Fleming stared at him. "We won't just dump them into the ravine and leave them to rot. We'll make a regular grave out've it."

They came up to the mounted men, and

the two nearest them backed their horses to permit Sturges to enter the circle.

"All right, you people," he said to the homesteaders. "Get hitched up and climb up into your wagons." He turned to Fleming. "You know where the place is, don't you? Then suppose you get your horse and lead the way? The boys and me will follow along behind the wagons."

Fleming hesitated for a moment. Then with a shake of his head and an unhappy heaviness inside of him, he squeezed through between two wagons and, emerging on the other side of the train, stopped again and looked about. There was no sign of his horse. He could hear the stamp of a horse's hoof in the darkened barn just a dozen steps away, and he stalked inside. It was so gloomily dark in there, it took him a minute or so to accustom his eyes to the darkness. Then he made out the form of a horse standing in one of the low partitioned stalls at the far end.

"All right, Brownie," he said crossly. "Come outta there and let's get going."

The horse stamped again, but he did not

back out of the stall. Frowning, Fleming started toward him. A shadowy figure rose up out of the darkness and wheeled after him, overtook him, and a gun butt came thudding down on the cattleman's head with a sickening thump. He gasped painfully and sagged at the knees; just as he was about to crumple, he was caught from behind by an arm that curled around his middle. His gun was yanked out of his holster, and he was half turned, shoved into a vacant stall opposite the occupied one, released and pushed. He fell face downward, caromed off a partition and slid brokenly to the hay-strewn floor. Swiftly the shadowy figure backed away, whirled around and disappeared into the cloaking darkness. The horse whinnied, but that was all the sound that came from the barn.

"Hey, Fleming!" It was Sturges' voice. "What d'you say?"

There was a brief silence. When there was no response to his call, Sturges appeared in the door and poked his head inside.

"How about it, Fleming?" he asked. "You're holding us up, you know."

The horse pawed the floor, scraped it with his hoof, and Sturges took a couple of sauntering steps into the barn, stopped again, and said:

"Aw, come on, willyuh, Fleming? We wanna put the torch to this place same's we did to the house, and you're holdin' us up."

He turned his head when he thought he heard movement somewhere behind him. It was too late. The hard, uncompromising muzzle of a gun collided with his spine, jarring him and making him stiffen, and a voice hissed in his ear:

"Just one little peep outta you, Sturges, and I'll blow you apart."

The rancher gulped and swallowed hard. There was no need for him to wonder about the identity of the man who was holding the gun on him. It was Canavan. It had to be Canavan, and he knew that it was. A sickishness crept over him. He felt a little weak in the knees. He swallowed hard in an effort to down the lump that had formed in his throat. He winced when the muzzle dug deeper into him. His gun was jerked out of his holster, and his captor hissed at him again.

"Now listen to me, Sturges, and listen good. You're gonna walk to the doorway and stand there and you're gonna tell those miserable, mangy lookin' critters waiting for you outside that this is as far as you're gonna go with the nesters tonight. Tell them that you and Fleming have talked it over and you've decided you've thrown enough of a scare into the nesters, and that you're satisfied for now. Tell them to pick up the dead and head for home with them and that you'll be along a little later on. Got that?"

There was no reply.

Annoyed with him, Canavan jabbed his gun viciously into Sturges' back.

"Well?" he demanded.

"I'll . . . I'll tell them."

"See that you do," Canavan gritted at Sturges. He prodded the man with his gun, turned with him, pushed him when he seemed hesitant, and dogging the cattleman's steps, followed him doorward, still maintaining the menacing pressure of his gun on him. "Make it sound natural," Canavan whispered over Sturges' shoulder. "And just because I haven't mentioned it up to now, don't get any ideas and try anything. Because if you do, you won't have a chance to wish you hadn't."

"I . . . I won't try anything."

"You'd better not," Canavan told him grimly, "if you want to stay alive."

They halted shortly when Canavan plucked at Sturges' shirt, stopping him just inside the middle of the doorway with the deep darkness from within the barn backgrounding Sturges and shielding Canavan. But the lined-up wagons stood between them and the mounted men, and Canavan had to herd Sturges outside. Driving the cattleman ahead of him, he forced him to march along the line till they came to a foot or two wide gap between a couple of wagons, and halted him there, made him stand there long enough for Canavan to get a quick look at the house. The fire was still burning. However, there was little left of the house, just one upright corner around which a vine of flame was curled. Having consumed the furniture and failing to find anything else of a substantial nature to feed on, the fire appeared to be burning itself out. There was lantern light on the far side of the barrier, and Canavan stepped back from him and crouched down behind a high rear wheel with his gun still pointed at Sturges.

"All right," he hissed at the rancher. "Speak your piece and make it good."

Sturges made a throaty sound.

"Men," he began, and Canavan, stealing a guarded look through the wheel's spokes, saw heads and faces turn in Sturges' direction. "Fleming and me have had a little talk, and we've decided that this will do for tonight. We've showed the nesters we mean business, and they oughta be able to figure out for themselves what they'll be in for if we have to come after them again. So you men can go home now." He stopped and just as Canavan was about to prod him again, to remind him that he had forgotten something, he added: "Oh, yeah. Pick up the dead on the other side of the wall and take them with you. Lay th'm out in the tool shed for the time being. I'll be along a little later on and we'll figure out then what to do with them."

For a moment there was no reaction to his announcement, no sound save the aimless pawing of hoofs on the churned-up ground. Then it came, a sudden murmur of relief from the homesteaders; it swelled almost at once and became a jumble of happy and excited voices, all talking at the same time. The mounted men began to back their horses. Thumping, drumming hoofs competed briefly with the jabbering voices, then they backgrounded them as the horsemen rode away. Then, someone, a man, shouldered his way through the laughing, milling homesteaders, strode up to the wagons to where Sturges was standing, and Canavan, raising up a bit, heard the man say:

"Thanks, Sturges."

Canavan recognized the voice. It was Reuben Fisher's.

"Thanks for stopping things when you

did," Fisher continued. "I think that was a good sign, that despite Canavan's belief that the only way to resolve differences is by force and violence, that you don't agree with that theory any more than I do. I'm of the opinion that if he hadn't taken it upon himself to interfere in matters that didn't concern him, there wouldn't have been any trouble between us. I think that if you and I were able to sit down together and talk things over, we could come up with a peaceful and satisfactory solution to our differences. Are you willing to try?"

There was no answer from Sturges.

"I asked if you were willing to try," Fisher repeated.

There was massed movement among the homesteaders, an indication that they were crowding forward around Fisher in order to hear better. Suddenly, Sturges, propelled from behind, came bursting through the gap. He collided head on with the surprised and unprepared Fisher, trampled him too, before the homesteader, raising his hands instinctively to hold him off, gave ground to him. Backing off a little, crowding into the people who had gathered around him, Fisher saw a tall figure come through the gap, and holstering his gun, come up next to Sturges. The latter, breathing hard, half turned his head and gave Canavan a hard look, but Canavan disregarded it.

"You don't learn, do you, Reuben?" Canavan chided Fisher. "You still think you can make friends of people who hate your guts, don't you? And you thought that was a good sign, huh, when Sturges called off his dogs and sent them home? I hate to disillusion you, Reuben, but Sturges didn't do that out've the goodness of his heart. I don't think he was either one, goodness or heart. It happened that I was holding my gun on him, and he did and said what I told him, and not for any other reason."

Canavan's eyes, ranging around the circle of faces turned to him, sought Molly. He found her standing off to a side, with young Johnny in front of her, and her arms curled protectively around him. A man came trudging up with three light lanterns swinging from each hand; he was relieved of them, and those who took them from him held up the lanterns, lighting up the spot.

"Couple o' you men go get Fleming," Canavan directed. "You'll find him in the barn, layin' in one of the stalls, sleeping off a headache. Bring him out here."

Two homesteaders, one of them holding a lantern aloft about shoulder high, and leading the way a stride ahead of his companion, rounded the first wagon in the line and disappeared behind it. Minutes passed, then there were loud voices, one of them raised in protest, from the direction of the barn. Then the two men returned supporting Fleming between them, hatless, a little rubbery legged, and holding one hand to his head. They led him up to Canavan. He swayed a bit, but he steadied himself almost at once, lifted his eyes to Canavan; he seemed to experience some difficulty getting them focused properly. When he did, he stared at Canavan a little open-mouthed. He wiped his mouth with the back of his hand.

"Where were you and Sturges gonna take these people?" Canavan asked him.

"Out a ways on the range," Sturges said before Fleming could answer.

"I asked him," Canavan said coldly to Sturges. "Not you. What were you gonna do with them, Fleming, once you got them out there?"

"Just leave them there," Sturges said, quickly again.

Canavan looked annoyed.

"What were you gonna do with them, Fleming?" he asked again, ignoring Sturges' reply. "And don't tell me you were gonna leave them there, and that that was all you were gonna do."

Fleming did not answer. Canavan stepped past Sturges, suddenly lunged and grabbed Fleming by the shirt front and with an upward heave of his arm hauled him up on his toes. With his face but inches from Fleming's, he raged at him:

"I want an answer, and I want an honest one, and if I have to beat it out've you, I will. But whether I do or not, that's up to you. Now will you talk, or d'you want me to make you?"

"We . . . we weren't gonna take them out

there at all," Fleming faltered. "We were gonna take them out to Sleigers old place."

"What's out there?"

"A ravine."

"All right. And then?" Canavan demanded, tightening his grip on Fleming's shirt.

"I . . . I was against the idea," Fleming protested wildly. "If we'da killed them all in a fight, that woulda been one thing. But to kill them in cold blood . . ."

"And then dump them into the ravine."

"Yes. That was what Sturges wanted to do."

"What I wanted to do?" Sturges yelled. "Why, you wall-eyed, yeller-bellied liar, that was your idea right from the beginning. I oughta punch you right smack . . ."

Canavan flung Fleming away, sent him reeling back, and he fell heavily at the feet of the two homesteaders. Then Canavan whirled around, struck Sturges savagely in the face, and the cattleman staggered backward, collided jarringly with the wagon, and slid down on his backside. Canavan leaped after him, bent down and dragged him up again, slammed him back against the wagon, and held him there. Sturges' eyes were glassy and his lips blood-flecked. There was a deepening yellowish and greenish welt on his cheek; it stood out above the crimson imprint, already beginning to fade, of Canavan's knuckles. Canavan held him with one hand and waved a big fist in his face.

"Now it's your turn to talk, Mister," he told Sturges, whose eyes were beginning to clear. "And you'd better talk a lot and fast. You wouldn't give Fleming a chance to answer, kept hornin' in on him when I wanted to hear what he had to say. But now that I've heard all I wanted from him, I'm ready to listen to you. So talk, Mister. But before you do, I'm gonna tell you something. I knew all about the raid you and your side-partner over there were cookin' up." Sturges glanced around. The two homesteaders had helped him to his feet. "Embree tipped me off. Then he tried to talk me into going after you and killing you, that is before the raid came off, figuring that that would make the others in on it decide to call it off. What I want to know now is what happened between you and Embree that made him want you killed off?"

"I dunno, Canavan. Honest, I don't. Y'see, when Pierce, the feller in charge of the Land Office . . ."

"I know what his job was."

"Well, when he told us there wasn't anything we could do about the nesters filin' on our grazing lands, we went to see Embree about it." Canavan scoffed. "He was the one who came up with the idea for the raid. On top o' that, he said we didn't have anything to worry about once we got rid of the nesters. If a marshal showed up and started askin' questions and did any lookin' into things. Embree said he'd cover up for us, and we'd be in the clear."

"That was real nice of him, wasn't it? Then how come after he told you that, he turned around and tried to get you killed off?"

"Y'got me, Canavan. I'm blamed if I can tell you."

"I think you can, Sturges. Fact is, I know you can. What's more, I think you two had a falling out over something and it had to do with Pierce's killing. Now what d'you think of that?"

Sturges didn't answer.

"Well?" Canavan demanded. "You lose your tongue alluva suddan?"

"It had something to do with Pierce," Sturges finally and reluctantly admitted. "That is, in a way."

"That's what I thought."

"The feller who killed Pierce was one o' my hands."

"I know. And his name was Waco."

"But I didn't have anything to do with it," Sturges protested. "That's a fact. I didn't know what Waco was up to, or anything."

"Y'mean you want me to believe that Waco took it on himself to go after Pierce and kill him if he had to, to get Pierce's record book away from him so that the nesters wouldn't have any official proof of their claims? Then you and the other cattlemen could've jumped in and registered your claims and nobody could have stopped you. You'd have had your lands back and that would have been that."

Sturges made no response.

"No go, Sturges," Canavan said with a shake of his head. "I wouldn't go for that story no matter what. I don't believe it, not one little bit of it either. I think it's a lie from beginning to end. I think you put Waco up to killing Pierce just as I think it was your idea, not Fleming's, to kill every one o' these people. You're no good, Sturges. You're bad, downright bad. And the sooner something's done about you, the better."

He released the rancher, stepped back and turned away from him, looked at the two homesteaders who were standing just beyond Fleming.

"Their horses oughta be somewhere around here," he told them. "Wanna see if you fellers can round them up?"

"Sure," one of the men answered.

His companion followed him away.

"What are you going t'do with them, Canavan?" another homesteader asked.

Canavan turned to him.

"Hand them over to the law," he replied.

"What good'll that do?" the man asked. "If the sheriff is workin' hand-in-hand with the cattlemen . . ."

"I don't mean the sheriff. He isn't any better than they are."

"Oh," the homesteader said, obviously relieved.

"I mean the gover'ment," Canavan explained. "The United States Gover'ment. They'll know what to do with them, 'specially with Mister Sturges."

"Uh-huh. Now there's just this last thing, and it's got me kinda worried."

"What is it?"

"The Land Office record book. If that's gone, what proof will there be that our claims were registered and that we really own what we filed on?"

"I don't think you have anything to worry about on that score."

"You mean the book's safe?"

Canavan nodded gravely.

"Yes," he said. "And when I hand over Sturges and Fleming, I'll turn over the book too."

11

IT was two days later, the time about four o'clock in the afternoon. Giffy appeared in the open doorway of the office, and backed against the door jamb. He ranged his gaze upstreet, hastily shaded his eyes with his hand because the sun was strong and glary. After a bit, he turned his head and looked downstreet. There was little activity; what little there was did not hold his interest or attention very long. With a deep, wearied sigh, he straightened up, straddled the metal threshold strip, and glanced inside. The sheriff, wearing a frowning and thoughtful expression on his face, sat slope-shouldered at his desk, hunched over his folded arms, and stared moodily into empty space.

"I'm beginning to think we mighta made a mistake," Giffy began. "Maybe we shoulda gone out to that Fisher feller's place anyway. We wouldn't have had to let on that we knew anything about the raid. Just that we'd heard shooting and got to wondering about it and rode out to see what we could find out. Then we would have known what really happened out there the other night."

There was no answer. Embree didn't even look up.

"This way," the deputy continued, "all we know is what we've been told, and not by anybody who mighta known everything that happened. We know the raid came off, that alluva sudden, just when Sturges had the nesters right where he wanted them, when he coulda done anything he wanted with them, wiped them out one, two, three, he got a change o' heart, called the raid off, and sent his bunch home. He told his crew he'd follow them home, but now it's two days later and they're still waiting for him to show up there. Same thing goes for Fleming. He hasn't showed up at his place yet either. Now what d'you suppose could have happened to Sturges an' Fleming?"

"I dunno, Giff," the sheriff replied, sitting up and squaring back in his chair.

"Haven't any idea. But you know what I hope has happened to them."

Giffy grinned fleetingly.

"Another thing that's got me wondering," he went on shortly, "is what coulda happened to Canavan? We both saw him go tearing outta here the night of the raid. But nobody's said anything about seeing him anywhere after he left here. Only way I can figure it is that when he got to Fisher's place and he saw what was going on there, Sturges' bunch swarming all over the nesters, he decided there wasn't any point in stayin' there and letting the cattlemen get their hands on him along with the others, and maybe killing him same's he figured they might do to the nesters. So he turned around and high-tailed it away from there without anybody seein' him come or go."

Embree voiced no opinion of his own. He grunted, but Giffy had no way of interpreting it, of knowing whether it was an affirmative sign or an indication that the sheriff didn't think too highly of Giffy's explanation of Canavan's disappearance. The deputy looked at him oddly.

"Beats me how you can be bustin' with curiosity and still do nothing to satisfy it," he said.

"It isn't easy, Giff, believe me," Embree told him wryly. "But since we aren't supposed to know there was a raid, if we were to ride to Fisher's place and make out that we were just checkin' around, somebody might get suspicious, and it wouldn't do us any good. If we stay put here and somebody should stop by and ask me if I heard the shooting the other night, I don't aim to say I didn't. I'm gonna say 'course I heard it. But because I didn't think it meant anything, I didn't do anything about it. Around these parts, it isn't anything out've the ordinary for somebody to get himself likkered up and suddenly think shadows are men and that they're after him and for him to cut loose at them with his gun. That's gonna be the way I aim to explain it. That we didn't go see what it was about."

"I see."

"So we'll stay put here, like I said, and wait for somebody who really knows what happened out at that nester's place to come

288

by and tell us. And then if I think it might be the right thing for us to do, we'll ride out to Fisher's. Till then though, we don't do anything, because what we don't know can't hurt us."

Giffy's thick shoulders lifted in a shrug.

"You're the boss," he said. "And if that's the way you want to play it, it's all right with me."

Hoofs drummed upstreet, and Giffy poked his head out again.

"Well, what d'you know!" he said after a moment's hard staring. "It's Coley Nye."

"Oh?"

"This is the first time he's been around since he tangled with Canavan and got his wrist busted. He's got some feller with him."

Embree climbed stiffly to his feet, hitched up his pants, trudged heavily to the doorway and peered out.

"Pulling up in front of the saloon," he observed.

"Yeah," Giffy said. "Sun's so blamed strong, I can't tell much by looking at the feller with Coley. He look familiar to you?"

"Nope," the sheriff said. "Don't think I've ever seen him before."

"They're getting down off their horses. Oh, now I can see them better. Skinny feller and kinda lanky. Kinda dark-faced too. Wears his gun low, almost like Canavan does."

"Like a lot of others do too," Embree said.

He turned on his heel and trudged back to his chair. As he slumped down in it on the tail of his spine, Giffy looked around at him and said:

"They just went inside."

"Good for them."

Giffy turned in the doorway and came striding back to the desk, leaned over it and said:

"Wouldn't it be something if it turned out that Sturges an' Fleming are dead, and for Canavan to come along now and for Nye to kill him? Then we'd really have nothing to worry about. All the troublemakers would be gone."

"That's what I've been hoping for," Embree answered, lifting his eyes to his deputy. "The way I've been hoping that things would work out."

"Maybe they will. Things have a way of working themselves out, you know. Maybe this is one o' those times."

"I'm willing," the sheriff said.

His chair squeaked as he burrowed back in it. Giffy walked to the doorway. Suddenly he said:

"Well, I'll be damned! Double damned!"

"Don't tell me they're working themselves out already?" Embree said chidingly.

"You'd better c'mere and see for yourself."

"See what for myself?"

Giffy looked at Embree over his shoulder.

"You believe in miracles?" he asked.

"Nope," the sheriff answered.

"You'd better," Giffy told him. "Because one's happening right now. Y'know who's coming up the street?"

"Nope. Who?"

"Down the street, I mean."

"Up or down, it doesn't matter. Who is it?"

"Canavan!"

Embree never moved faster. The excitement in Giffy's manner and voice had communicated itself to him. He fairly leaped out of his chair; he was across the office floor in a single, bounding stride. The chair, flung away, skidded backward and collided with the wall behind the desk and caromed off and spun around.

"Now do you believe in miracles?" Giffy wanted to know.

The sheriff did not answer. His wide eyes were fixed on the approaching Canavan, holding on him as he came downstreet at a trot. He watched Canavan come abreast of the saloon and then pass it. But then movement on the veranda caught Embree's eye and he stole a quick look in its direction. The stranger who had ridden into town with Coley Nye had come out on the veranda. They heard him yell:

"Canavan, you son-uva-bitch!"

Embree gulped and swallowed hard.

Canavan pulled up, twisted around and looked back. The lanky man came down the steps to the walk. He stood facing Canavan, a little spread-legged, with his right hand on his gun butt. When Giffy moved out of the doorway, Embree followed him; when Giffy started up the street at a jog, the sheriff was right behind him. When they neared Canavan, Giffy slowed his step, panted to a stop, and Embree bumped into him. Giffy, sensing that something intensely dramatic was about to happen, and gripped by its breathtaking possibilities, was too absorbed and much too excited to notice. When he pushed backward to get out of range of an errant shot, Embree gave way, backed with him into the doorway of a vacant store. They saw a white-aproned figure, Tuck Wells, appear on the saloon veranda, saw a towering man, Coley Nye, join him.

"Well, well, well!" they heard Canavan say and their heads jerked. "Had to look twice to make sure it was you, Deglin. When did they let you out?"

"They didn't. I broke out," was the curt

reply. "Kinda surprised to see me, huh, you redheaded bastid?"

Canavan laughed lightly and said:

"Yeah, I suppose I am. Still, you have to expect a bad penny to keep poppin' up every now and then."

"I told you when you took me in that I'd get you some day, didn't I? That I'd find you no matter where you might be?"

"Did you tell me that? Guess I must've forgotten over the years."

"I'm gonna kill you, Canavan."

"You can try," Canavan answered evenly. "But I wouldn't bet on your chances. Not if you aren't any handier now with a gun than you were years ago. The way I remember it, that cattleman whose killing you went up for, you shot in the back. You weren't good enough to take him face-to-face."

"That's a lie!" Deglin screamed, reddening. But he checked himself in almost the same instant, and controlling his anger, said with surprising calm: "Had a couple o' friends of mine keeping a lookout for you. They were gonna keep me posted on where you were. When I didn't hear from them, I took it to mean it just happened that you didn't hit the same places they did. But I knew that one day you would. Then alluva sudden I got word that you were hangin' around Cuero. I busted out've prison and headed this way, hoping for only one thing, that you'd still be here when I got here. I ran into somebody who was lookin' to hire a gun to take care of you. We made a deal right off. Now, instead of killing you just for the satisfaction I'm gonna get out've it, out've seeing you layin' in your own rotten blood, I'm gonna get paid for killing you. Get down off your horse," Deglin ordered, and his hand tightened around his gun butt.

"All right," Canavan said, and he climbed down from the mare.

He patted her, spoke to her, and she trotted away. Embree's eyes followed her. He saw her stop again some forty or fifty feet farther down the street, saw her push her way in between two idling, head-bowed horses that were tied up at a hitch rail. Swiftly the sheriff's gaze reversed itself and came racing back to hold on Canavan.

"All right, Deglin," he heard Canavan say. "I'm down. What do we do now?"

"Here it comes," Giffy whispered to Embree excitedly.

They saw Deglin's right arm jerk, saw his body half twist as he yanked out his gun. But before he could snap it upward for a shot, there was an overpowering roar of gunfire, two, three swift shots, that beat against their ears deafeningly and made them wince. They looked in Canavan's direction, saw a thin wisp of blue smoke curling gently around him, saw it lift and dissolve. When they took their eyes from him and shot another look at Deglin, they stared even wider-eyed than before. He was on his hands and knees, half turned away from Canavan, flung around by the staggering impact of the bullets that had slammed into his body, with his bowed head just above the curb and sinking lower and lower. His body arched forward, and he slid over the curb, face downward in the gutter.

"That's that," Giffy said aloud. "That's one feller who won't have to worry about going back and serving out his time."

Slowly Canavan straightened up. He glanced at the two lawmen, turned his back on them, reloaded his gun as he sauntered to the curb, stepped up on the walk and started for the saloon. Embree's gaze ranged ahead of Canavan. As it focused on the saloon, Tuck Wells came down the steps and backed off. Embree's eyes lifted. He could see Coley Nye standing in the shadows of the doorway. Suddenly Nye stepped out on the veranda. His gun flashed in his hand, and roared twice. The sheriff blinked. When he looked again, Nye had retreated to the doorway. Canavan halted some fifteen or twenty feet from the saloon, and with his gun raised, waited for Nye to take another shot at him. His wait was a short one, probably no more than half a minute. Nye stepped out again, this time in full view, to the head of the steps. Canavan and he fired at the same time, their shots blending together into a single clap of man-made thunder. Embree, shuttling his gaze between the two, stared a little when he saw Canavan's hat spin around on the walk, flutter and fall limply at his feet. When he heard a curious thump, heard it repeated, he looked saloonward wonderingly. He saw Nye roll down the steps and strike the planked walk with a hollow, dust-raising thud and come to a full stop when his body rolled against one of Deglin's feet, which were propped up, toes downward, on the curb.

Canavan stood motionlessly, a little crouched, with his gun still levelled and still holding on the fallen cattleman as the dust began to settle around him. But after a moment or two, when Nye did not stir, Canavan reached down with his free hand and picked up his hat. Slowly, still watchful though, he began to back off from Nye. Slowly too he came erect, holstered his gun, turned on his heel and marched down-street. When he stopped and whistled, there was an immediate response; the mare shrilled, backed away from the rail, wheeled and came clattering up to him. She nuzzled him and when he patted her, she whinnied happily. He climbed up on her and rode away, the fleet mare's hoofs drumming a swift beat as she carried him up the street and out of town.

For a moment or two the fading echoes of the gunfire hung in the air, then it was gone. People emerged from stores and dwellings and from alleys. The women stood about in little groups, talking among themselves in low, almost awed tones, and half turned their backs on the dead bodies that lay in front of the saloon. Despite their reluctance to look, their eyes were drawn to them. The menfolk gathered around Nye and Deglin, and moved to meet Embree and Giffy when the lawmen crossed the street. Embree bent over Deglin, peered hard at him and straightened up again; he bent a little lower over Nye. He looked up when Giffy joined him, stood up, and said a little scornfully:

"Some miracle, all right. And if this is what you mean by things working themselves out . . ."

He didn't finish. He shouldered Giffy out of his way and stalked off.

It was some two miles outside of Cuero that Canavan heard the beat of oncoming horses. He pulled back on the reins, slowed

Aggie to a trot. Presently two horsemen came into view; Canavan eyed them, and recognizing them, nudged Aggie into faster movement and rode on to meet them. They came together shortly, Canavan and two men who wore silver stars pinned to their shirt pockets, and eased themselves in their saddles.

"Get them?" Canavan asked.

"Yeah, sure," one of the men answered. "Got full statements from all three of them. Weber didn't like the idea at first, arguing that he didn't have anything to do with the raid. But then he gave in, told us everything he knew—that is, what Fleming had told him. Booth and Kiley needed a little prodding, but they finally opened up and came through with what we wanted of them. Add their statements to Fleming's and we've got all we need to put Sturges and Embree away for a long, long time. What's that, Red?"

He raised up a little and peered at Canavan's hat, and pointed to something in its crown.

"Bullet hole," the latter answered

calmly. "Something I picked up in my travels."

Dave sank down again.

"Must've just picked it up then," was his dry response. "You didn't have it this morning."

"You notice too much, Dave," Canavan told him. "One of you gonna stay around Cuero till a new sheriff takes over for Embree?"

"That's Steve's assignment," Dave said. "My job's to pick up Embree and bring him in. Then I'm heading south. Things have gotten a little outta hand in a couple of border towns, and the locals have been hollering for help. So I'm it. Embree's around where I can find him, isn't he?"

Canavan nodded.

"Oh, before I forget this," he said. "If there's a want out for somebody named Deglin . . ."

"There is," the second horseman, the man named Steve, said, interrupting Canavan. "Busted out of Huntsville after killing a guard. So they'd like an awful lot to get him back."

"Strike him off your list."

"Mean there's no point looking for him?"

"'Fraid not, Steve."

"I see. Dead, is he?"

"Dead as he'll ever be."

"Cause of death?"

"Oh, just say gunshot wound. That will cover it."

"And where it asks 'Circumstances,' what do I say?"

"Unknown," Canavan said quietly.

"Mightn't it be even better for Steve's report to say it was suicide?" Dave asked, glancing again at the bullet hole in Canavan's hat.

Canavan met Dave's eyes.

"It probably would be at that, because that's about what it amounted to."

"Then that's what I'll say," Steve said.

"Meant to tell you this sooner, Red," Dave began, and Canavan's eyes held on him again. "Started to this morning, but something else came up and I didn't get back to it. I saw Cap McDermott a couple of weeks ago."

"Oh?"

"He's getting old fast now. Coming to the end of the trail."

"But he's feeling all right though, isn't he?"

"So he says. He asked for you. Wanted to know if I ever run into you. He still talks about you. I heard him telling a couple o' new Rangers 'bout what a lawman you were, and to do things the way you did. You'd make him feel awfully good, Red, if once in a while, when you get a chance that is, you'd sit yourself down somewhere and get off a letter to him. You wouldn't have to tell him too much. Just that you're all right. He'd be tickled to death to hear from you."

Canavan made no response.

"You know as well as I do," Dave blurted out, "that he didn't let you go because he wanted to. He had to."

"I know."

"Then when you get a chance . . ."

"I'll write to him."

Dave nodded and held out his hand to Canavan. The latter gripped it.

"So long, Red."

"So long, Dave."

Steve leaned forward and shook hands with Canavan too, then the three men backed their horses away.

"Good luck, Red," Dave called over his shoulder as he wheeled after Steve.

Canavan acknowledged with a half-salute that would have made Tuck Wells beam, nudged Aggie with his knees and rode away. He looked back just once. There was no sign of the two Rangers. Heavily, he settled himself in the saddle.

Wheeling into the cut-through and slowing Aggie to a trot, Canavan glanced at the barrier as he rode along it, and wondered if the homesteaders had continued extending it or if they had abandoned work on it. They had probably stopped, he told himself. But he didn't blame them. Having to live out of the limited and uncomfortable confines of wagons that were already overloaded with household goods and personal belongings, completely uncertain about what the future held in store for them, was enough to discourage anyone, even the hardiest and the most determined. As he neared the barn, so drab looking and so badly in need of a painting, and the lined-up wagons in front of it, he raised up a little in his stirrups and ranged his gaze ahead eagerly. The site on which the house had stood was fire-blackened and desolate looking. Only one corner upright remained, half burned off, but still standing as though in majestic defiance. There was no one about, no sound of anyone. The silence and the smell of fire which still hung in the air was depressing. Then as he came abreast of the wagons and drew rein, there was a glad cry and he pulled up at once. Johnny Fisher crawled out from underneath one of the wagons, scrambled to his feet and ran to him.

"You've come back!" the boy cried happily. "You've come back!"

Canavan reached down for him, lifted him and settled him sideways in front of him.

"They said we'd never see you again," Johnny told him.

"Guess this proves they were wrong,

doesn't it? Where is everybody, Johnny?"

"Working."

Canavan climbed down, lifted the boy into the saddle, pushed the reins into his chubby hands and asked:

"Want to ride her around for a minute, while I get something from the barn?"

"Oh, sure!"

"Just watch it though," Canavan cautioned him.

"You mean I shouldn't make her run?"

"That's the idea," Canavan answered gravely.

He watched the boy ride away, saw Aggie turn her head and level a questioning look at Johnny, then he squeezed through between two wagons and trudged into the barn. Minutes later when he emerged with his saddlebags slung over his left shoulder and his blanket roll caught up under his right arm, Molly Fisher suddenly appeared in front of him, and he stopped abruptly.

"Oh," he said. "Hello."

"You're . . . you're leaving us?" she faltered.

"That's right, Molly."

"You were going without saying goodbye to me?"

"I thought that was the way you wanted it."

Her eyes probed his face.

"Where . . . where are you going?" she asked.

"To California."

"But you'll come back again one day, won't you?"

"No, Molly."

Tears came into her eyes.

"Then I'll never see you again?"

He shook his head.

"I know it was selfish of me, but I hoped and prayed you'd never want to leave us," she told him. "Couldn't you stay on, if not here with us, then somewhere close by, so that I might see you even if only once in a while? Just to know that you're always within reach . . ."

"It wouldn't be good, Molly."

"Then take me with you!"

She reached for his hand, found it and clung to it with both of hers.

"Take me with you, Johnny!" she begged him.

He looked down into her face, smiled a little sadly at her.

"Remember what you told me that time in the hotel?" he asked her. "When I told you how much I wanted you, and how I wanted you to go 'way with me? 'I'm married to Reuben. I'm the mother of his child,' you told me. 'If I were to walk out on them now, when they both need me so, I'd never be able to live with myself. As time went on,' you said, 'I'd hate myself for what I had done, and I'd hate you too for having been a party to it.' I've never forgotten that, Molly, because you were so right. It wouldn't have worked out, and it wouldn't work out now either."

She sobbed softly and bowed her head against his chest.

"And for me to stay around, not right here because I couldn't do that any longer, but somewhere else around Cuero, that wouldn't be good either. That's why I've made up my mind to go. Maybe with me gone and things settling down around here, you'll have so much to do, so much to think about and plan for, you won't have time to think about me. You'll forget me after a while, and you'll find you can be happy with Reuben all over again. He's a stubborn cuss, Molly, but he's a good man, and a decent one. Give him time and he'll catch on to the ways of the people around here, and he'll be an even better man for it."

The plod of approaching hoofs reached them.

"It's Johnny," Canavan said. "You don't want him to see you crying, do you?"

Quickly Molly dried her eyes. When she turned and led the way around the first wagon, Canavan trooped after her. Johnny rode up to them.

"How was it?" Canavan asked him.

"Gee, I wish she was mine!"

"Maybe you'll have one just like her some day."

He handed Molly his blanket roll and reached for the boy, curled his arm around him and lifted him off. He hoisted his bags, draped them over Aggie's back, took the roll from Molly and strapped it on behind the saddle. He chucked Johnny under the chin and the laughing boy retreated to his mother's side. Canavan climbed up, settled himself in the saddle, winked at Johnny, and rode away. He looked back once, when he was nearing the beginning of the cut-through and the road just beyond it. Molly was on her knees, she had Johnny in her arms and she was holding him tight against her. Canavan had to swallow hard to down the lump that arose in his throat.

Despite the fading daylight and the lengthening shadows, Canavan recognized the cumbersome, swaying wagon that was rumbling along ahead of him. He whacked Aggie on the rump and the surprised mare bounded away, flashed past the wagon in such a burst of speed that it made the wagon appear to be standing still.

"Canavan!"

It was as he had expected, Doreen Gregg's voice. But he gave no sign that he had heard her. Aggie's pounding hoofs drowned out her voice when she called after him a second time. Swiftly the mare

310

widened the gap between them. When the crunching grind of the wheels and the plod of the team's hoofs had died away behind them, Canavan slowed Aggie to a lope and rode on into the gathering dusk.

THE END

*Other titles in the
Linford Western Library:*

FARGO: MASSACRE RIVER
by John Benteen

Fargo spurred his horse to the edge of the road. Its right hind hoof slipped perilously over the edge as he forced it around the wagon. Ahead he saw Jade Ching riding hard, bent low in her saddle. Fargo rammed home his spurs and drove his mount up to her. The ambushers up ahead had now blocked the road. Fargo's convoy was a jumble, a perfect target for the insurgents' weapons!

SUNDANCE:
DEATH IN THE LAVA
by John Benteen

The land echoed with the thundering hoofs of Modoc ponies. In minutes they swooped down and captured the wagon train and its cargo of gold. But now the halfbreed they called Sundance was going after it, and he swore nothing would stand in his way—not Indian savagery of the vicious gunfighters of the town named Hell.

GUNS OF FURY
by Ernest Haycox

Dane Starr, alias Dan Smith, wanted to close the door on his past and hang up his guns, but people wouldn't let him. Good men wanted him to settle their scores for them. Bad men thought they were faster and itched to prove it. Starr had to keep killing just to stay alive.

FARGO: PANAMA GOLD
by John Benteen

A soldier of fortune named Cleve Buckner was recruiting an army of killers, gunmen and deserters from all over Central America. With foreign money behind him, Buckner was going to destroy the Panama Canal before it could be completed. Fargo's job was to stop Buckner—and to eliminate him once and for all!

HELL RIDERS
by Steve Mensing

Outlaw Wade Walker's kid brother, Duane, was locked up in the Silver City jail facing a rope at dawn. When Wade rode into town the sheriff knew trouble had already begun. Wade was a ruthless outlaw, but he was smart, and he had vowed to have his brother out of jail before morning!

DESERT OF THE DAMNED
by Nelson Nye

The law was after him for the murder of a marshal—a murder he didn't commit. Breen was after him for revenge—and Breen wouldn't stop at anything . . . blackmail, a frameup . . . or murder. He was desperate now and vowed to find a way out—or make one.